ANNIEDOTES

ELIZABETH WILLIAMS

Gabriel
'Thank you for the music'

Libby
Christmas 2005

PublishBritannica
London   Baltimore

© 2003 by Elizabeth Williams.
All rights reserved. No part of this book may be reproduced, stored in a retrieval system, or transmitted in any form or by any means without the prior written permission of the publishers, except by a reviewer who may quote brief passages in a review to be printed in a newspaper, magazine, or journal.

First printing

ISBN: 1-4137-1170-7
PUBLISHED BY PUBLISHBRITANNICA
www.publishbritannica.com
London   Baltimore

Dedicated to the memory of my dear mother and father, Annie and Len Falkner

1 MURDI

He was only a small cat – black, silky and beautiful, seven weeks old, inquisitive in every way. He was part of our one parent family, loved, cared for and very special.

To be awakened one morning by his piercing cry was heart rending. The boys got to the bottom of the stairs before I did and there was Murdock, a terrorised tiny black ball, stuck in the small curls of the wrought iron staircase. The only way we were able to distinguish him from the ebony circle was via his white teeth, pink tongue and terrified green eyes.

Pulling the tiny fur ball was impossible, hampered by the fear of damaging his small organs or breaking his little legs. Chris tried with all his strength to pull apart the ironwork. Alex fretted and shouted. Mum panicked and called 999 at 5:45 am crying and really distressed. Unable to cope with hurting animals, she did her utmost to explain that her poor pussy was stuck! The rather bemused but patient operator took control.

Five minutes later the sharp bell of a fire engine sounded at the southern end of the road, awakening the neighbourhood. Mum opened the door to be greeted by three huge firemen in full uniform, each wearing a helmet and carrying a chopper.

"Trouble with your pussy, Madam?"

Mum in dressing gown, hair awry and tears pouring down her cheeks said, "Thank heavens you've come. He's stuck."

One huge booted foot crossed the threshold as Chris shouted, "Mum, he's out."

Smiling firemen marched down the path and back to the engine; one turned and smiled.

"Don't worry, mam."

Suddenly they were off in a northerly direction, full bells blaring. It was only 5:55 am.

As if this was not shame enough, the following weekend's local paper sported a front page article entitled 'Pussy Rescue', alerting the neighbours yet again to the scatty woman at no. 74.

2 CHITTY BB

In the year 2002, a piece of magic returned to London, this time as a stage musical 'Chitty Chitty Bang Bang'.

How many now thirty-somethings are paying to see this spectacular? Is there an equal number still traumatised by the fear of the child catcher?

At a recent family party I learned from my sons that I had used the 'child catcher' as a deterrent, or a means to end some misbehaviour.

"I wasn't that bad, was I?"

My 36-year-old son relayed that he still has a fear of the child catcher coming to get him.

"Mum, you even used the phone to pretend to call him to come and get us if we were naughty."

For goodness sake, I wasn't serious.

It worked though!

3 UNMENTIONABLES

Have you seen the 'blue blood' ads? I mean those for small pieces of white, almost oblong-shaped hygiene wear? Some have wings!

None of the adverts leave much to the imagination. There is so much choice; everything is so open and honest now with companies selling discreet pads for older women with a few 'plumbing' problems and thirty-somethings leaving tampon boxes on bathroom windowsills.

No so in the fifties!

Sanitary towels came in huge bulky packets that could never be hidden and were so embarrassingly obvious on the way back from Boots the Chemist!

When I was too young to know what they were but old enough to travel on the bus alone, Mum frequently sent me on a Sunday morning to the 'Little Wonder' corner shop in Morden. I had a note with some money in return for which I received a brown paper parcel or one made from yesterday's newspaper. I never knew what was in it.

A few years later I puzzled as to why Mum never had them in the house; she knew she would (hopefully) need them approximately every twenty-eight days. In later years I realised that she had to budget for them and maybe she went without something else to do so.

These women's necessities (whispered STs) were bulky with loops on each end that had to be fastened on to a sanitary belt, which was nearly always a horrible pink and chaffed your middle if you were overweight. It had two straps with metal fasteners, dangling just over the belly and the backside, to which the loops were affixed. (Forerunner of today's thong perhaps?)

One of the boys in our street was more curious than I was and perhaps not afraid of a clip round the ear. One day on the way back from Boots, he opened his brown paper parcel. Arriving home he rapped the knocker; Mum opened the door to be greeted by her cheeky son with one 'ST' draped over his head and one dangling from each ear! Never has a child been whisked from a doorstep and into a house with such speed.

Thank God for today's liberated women whom we assume also have 'blue blood'.

4 PASSED IT?

I'm a widow, now without my beautiful lover. He was 69 when he died and very able to fulfil me in every way. I am 62 – too young to lose my man, too needy in so many ways to be without him.

I sit here in south London on a lovely sunny afternoon missing him like crazy and watching the world go by. He was a fine figure of a man, bronzed, always in shorts, broad back and muscled arms, strengthened from heavy metal and wood work and gardening. His legs strong from swimming, cycling and brown from the Australian sun where he often spent the winter months.

I sit and remember him by our bedroom window, his white rear shining in the dark.

Suddenly back in Beckenham High Street, I find I am looking at other backsides; young men in shorts, in jeans, older men with brown legs riding on bikes!

There's life in the old gal yet!

5 CATCH YA' IN THE RYE

Divorce – a word used so freely these days. So many ways to make it possible to sever ties that were once joined by the wonder of love and the joy of partnership. We were not children of the sixties; we had children of that era. We were both married young, too young, and soon lost the bloom of early marriage and the passion that came with it. You wanted a divorce, so we planned to catch him by following him to Peckham where he parked his car on the Rye.

You couldn't afford to pay for a private detective, so we thought we would carry out 'DIY' surveillance. We were both short and tried to be inconspicuous with dark trousers, hooded duffle coats and scarves around the bottom of our faces (very 'B' movies).

We waited a respectable time; long enough we felt for back-seat antics to commence, although I often thought afterwards how difficult this must have been in the back of a bubble car. Did it have a back? We kept low to the ground, inching nearer. My heart was pounding, your stomach churning. Suddenly the car began rocking, accompanied by moans and squeals from inside. You were right beside the window, camera with flash poised to capture this 'tender' moment, ready for later development and onward transmission to your solicitor to await further developments.

My breathing became faster and louder; peering in the dark, leaning forward to get nearer the back window, the smell of the cold dank grass distracted me for a moment and caused me to slip, hitting my head on the back of the car. We both ducked in unison and you began to slowly creep around to the rear. Suddenly the car door sprung open and out he jumped, hitching up his trousers.

"Bleeding hell, there are a couple of kids watching us."

Have you ever had one of those nightmares where you are putting in all the effort to run and not appearing to move an inch?

"I'll get you, you little buggers," he shouted.

He chased after us and as I took a quick look back to see if you were keeping up, I saw he had a gun. Immediately the nightmare disappeared and Chris Chattaway sprang into my shoes.

The first shot rose into the air causing night to erupt and sleeping birds to wake. The second shot hit the side window of my old car as we jumped in almost simultaneously, screaming at our patient chauffeur to "get the hell out, he has a gun and is trying to kill us."

As we sped away I could not contain my emotion and terror, the first causing me to have a fit if hysteria, the second to pee myself.

We got no juicy pictures; you got your divorce without them. He carried on playing with his airgun, eventually shooting himself in the foot!

6 PART-TIME WORK

When you are a single mum and need to work, it must be preferable to be near home. I had two sons, thirteen and eight. I worked across the road; they had strict instructions what to do and definitely what not to do! Work started at 8 am. Number 1 son didn't wake until 8:30ish. Number 2 son was told not to go downstairs until No 1 arose.

Number 2's clothes were laid out for him.

Below is a list of phone calls received over a very short period during this manic and grey hair growing time in my life.

Number 2 Son

"Mum, bruv is still asleep. What do I do?"
"What's for breakfast?"
"Mum, can you please come home? I don't like these clothes."
"There's a bee in the bathroom."
"Mum, I feel sick."
"Mum, did you know that Stuart swore at school yesterday?"
"Mum, what does this say on the front page?"
"Can I go out in the field?"
"Mum, he won't let me practice my trumpet."

Number 1 Son

"Mum, can you come home? Bruv has set the kitchen on fire."

The saddest call was to come home because number 2 son's hamster had died. Moog (hamster, not son) had looked a little listless in the morning. Later that day number 2 found him outside his cage.

After I arrived home and picked up the hamster, I wondered if it had been dead when found by my son. Or perhaps it died a little later, as he had picked it up, screamed and thrown it over his shoulder.

If it were not dead at the outset, it would have been after it hit the wall, below which I found it after comforting my distressed offspring!

7 SECOND TIME AROUND

My friend called. He came with flowers, a smile and sweets for my sons. He took me dancing and for a meal. He brought me back safely, kissed me lightly on the lips and left.

The boys were asleep and our new baby, an eight week old jet-black kitten, mewed and fussed around my legs. I went to bed happy because of a fun evening and to feel the warmth, hopefully, of a man in my life again.

Lucky black cat!

A few days later, my man called again. He stayed very late. He fell in love with our kitten that equally adored him. As things progressed over a few more days, we tended to spend the last two hours of each day, after the boys had gone to bed and before he went home, 'courting' as my mother would call it! The passions were tempered by the thought of two sleeping boys above us and hampered by the advances of our kitten. Whatever position we attained, however close we became, soft black fur became the centre of attention, so much so that the love affair was almost between man and cat!

Murdock was the most amazing creature and moved with us all when we set up house together, the home in which we were together for 17 years.

He was a lucky black cat, living all of his nine lives to the full. He brought my man to me.

In April 2001 he had to be put to sleep, a terrible ordeal for my husband and I as we had gained so much from him over the years. Life was not quite the same without him and we missed him in every way. 17 years is a long life for a cat. 17 years was a wonderful life for my husband and me.

Sadly he went in November 2001 to join Murdock and I am left with no pet, no husband and a longing for this beautiful pair who had entered and enriched my life.

8 OVER THE EDGE

My husband, my soul mate, the love of my life died prematurely.

I coped. I arranged his funeral, celebration really. I got up each day, applied my make-up, did my hair and put on a mask for the outside world. I sold his car, had necessary work done on the house. I was executor for his will, dealt with solicitors, the taxmen and the small claims court. I comforted children, grandchildren and myself. I was strong. I bought a car. I survived – until today.

What was so huge that I completely lost control? What has caused loss of sleep, nightmares beyond belief? What has turned a brave woman into an irrational and neurotic mess?

ANTS!

I have bought no end of plastic boxes. All sweet things are in the fridge. I have bleached, cleaned, washed, sprayed and prayed.

And still they came.

This morning, teetering on the edge of a breakdown, I called Pest Control. I had to lock up the tortoise and keep next door's cats away for a couple of weeks. My bank balance is also a great deal lighter, but I CAN SLEEP TONIGHT!

9 'CORRYN'S REVENGE'

Three boys in 'Sunday go to chapel' clothes. I am Welsh Methodist, but I also sang in Bangor Cathedral choir, firstly because I got paid and secondly because it avoided a third visit to chapel on Sundays. These were war years, chapel was very important then. As my two brothers grew older, religion was replaced with other hobbies – drinking, smoking and girls.

Mam still went to chapel. She didn't like cigarettes, she loved a drop of whiskey in her later years and I feel it inappropriate to even think about the third hobby in the same context of my widowed Mam!

My brothers went to Australia; we drifted apart only to find each other many years later. At this time number 2 son had remarried and adopted Catholicism, much to Mam's chagrin. He was a radical convert, never missing Mass and crossing himself each time he passed the end of street where the church was situated.

When I visited him last year, he was really sick with Red-Back spider bites; two in fact had successively bitten his thigh. How? They were hiding under a seat in the church!

I can hear our dear mam from her reserved (tithed) heavenly seat saying something like, "I told you so," accompanied by a sentence about the retribution of her Welsh chapel God.

10 TOPLESS

Was I really fat? Big maybe, but curved and shapely. I was, however, fat in the head, lacking confidence and with low self-esteem. He came along and changed all that. He persuaded me to go swimming after about 28 years of hiding under tents at beaches and pretending to be allergic to the sun.

We planned a short holiday in Portugal.

"Buy a bikini," he said, "It would look good". I sometimes wonder if he had cataracts or tunnel vision. I bought a two-piece, shocking pink number, parading for days in front of my bedroom mirror.

"No one will know me in Portugal."

Our first day on the beach, a few rays and extra sun block later, he said, "Why don't you take off your top?"

"For goodness sake," I said, "It has taken 30 years to get it on and now you want me to take it off."

"Everyone does," he replied, "There aren't many people around."

Off it came and I spent the next twenty minutes flat against the sun bed, arms pinned motionless at the sides, terrified that the slightest move would unleash ripples and nipples.

He slept; the sun shone. I froze and the man arrived for the sun bed fee. "Hallo."

"Darling, the man wants the sun bed money." Nothing, no response. "Hey, the man wants some money." Just snores.

I slowly rose, walking to the other side of the bed, trying hard to prevent my breasts from moving left or right, north or south. I prayed my red face could be mistaken for early sunburn. Bending down to retrieve the sum from his wallet was tough, gravity versus buoyancy. I paid the young man – he smiled and left. I rushed back to my prone position on the sun bed, trying to avoid eye contact with fellow sun worshippers.

My head touched the pillow and my breasts fell into near armpit positions when the gravel-voiced joker lying next to me said, "Now that wasn't too hard, was it?"

11 DANCING IN THE DARK

What are the clubs like when the lights are on? I am sure the floors are washed, the tables wiped, glasses sparkled and CDs packed away in scratchproof covers. But look up at the ceiling – cobwebs? Dust? I can't say, I'm too old for clubbing, but I remember at 17 years of age we went dancing. Empire Leicester Square, the Orchid at Purley, Streatham Locarno, Hammersmith Palais on Friday/Saturday nights. There was another near Covent Garden, but I can't remember the name. All were very dusty in day light.

There was always a live band, excellent musicians with lots of work. At each of these places the dance floor fronted the stage, and there was a revolving globe in the ceiling that reflected what would now seem like very tame lighting. Nearly everyone smoked. The smell masked any other odours that emanated from hundreds of people jiving and writhing. There were chairs and tables around the edge of the dance floor. Behind these was a narrow red carpet, which separated the 'wall space'. This was where everyone congregated and it was really dark. It was a bit of a cattle market, a place to meet boys and girls.

Oh how I loved the music. Oh how I loved to dance. Oh how I wanted to dance. I was seventeen, fat, with hairy legs and a continental beauty moustached upper lip.

I went every week with my friend who always danced. Men fell over themselves to ask her. I stayed at the back feeling more and more conspicuous, tears hiding just behind my eyes, praying that someone would ask me. Did I appear desperate?

The last waltz, the big rush. Everyone wanted someone to dance with; everyone wanted someone to go home with or to at least make a date for same time next week. Nine times out of ten I wasn't asked. The tenth time it was what I considered to be a dirty old man who crushed my breasts and stuck his tongue in my ear. This was carried out whilst simultaneously pressing against my belly some unknown, but very hard object which he had hidden in his trousers. I was not introduced to one of these objects until much later!

At one time I danced with a wonderful black man. I was secretly terrified;

I had never met a black man before. I was also elated because he had asked me to dance. But over a two-year period, I had four dances.

The agony of standing by a dark wall, praying to be picked, still hangs as heavily in my heart as the cobwebs from the oppressive ceilings.

The pain of seventeen.

12 A LEGACY

Her brother died in the UK. As the nearest living relative she came from Canada to arrange the funeral and clear his home. She hadn't seen him for ten years since she had ceased to clean for him and emigrated. In that time he had deteriorated in health, and his mind had become a little addled. Perhaps it does when you live alone and don't talk much?

G was strong with big arms, a huge heart and a trailer, so he went to the house in Battersea to help empty the contents.

Who was the old and feeble man, a recluse who had died alone? He had obviously lived in one room at a time, gradually filling it and then moving on to the next. He never discarded anything. The house had been heated by a paraffin stove evident by the brown marks streaking the walls and ceiling, showing exactly where it had stood. When first opening the door, the smell of paraffin mixed with dust and other unpleasant odours smashed its way out into the daylight, with some of it finding its way to vacant and receptive nostrils, searing the insides and causing the bodies to shudder and try to avoid retching.

He had been a snazzy dresser in his day. Three piece, well cut dark suits were hanging from the walls. The hangers were attached to picture rails in every room and the hall; so many suits. Also in every room there were piles of newspapers dating back ten years. As the first pile was lifted to be disposed of, a bar of Cadbury's chocolate in its bright blue wrapper fell to the floor. G smiled to himself. "Another chocolate fan," he thought, "Never had time to eat it". How wrong he was! Each pile of newspaper revealed more and more wrapped chocolate bars carefully placed between the daily news; tens, fifties, hundreds of them! Why had the old man hidden them? Had he been obsessed? Had he been craving chocolate during the war years when sweets were rationed and feared the return of such restriction? We will never know.

The house gradually emptied and the trailer filled with sweet obsession, suited glory and old news. When all these strange possessions had been dumped, the trailer returned to be filled with ancient furniture, a grey rotting mattress and musty old pillows; moth-balled blankets and various bags of tired linen and towels.

At the bottom of the last drawer under old flannelette sheets was a heavy brown paper parcel. It was taken out, laid on the floor and carefully opened. The contents revealed items that may have given clues to what the uncle had done in his past days – a sawn off shotgun with a splendid, hard wood handle and an ornate carved silver barrel. This lethal weapon was accompanied by a Luger pistol and a box of ammunition.

The next thirty minutes lead to speculation and worry as to the use the uncle had put these. Plus, what was to be done with them? Everyone involved in the removal saw him in a different light and little shivers erupted whilst thoughts surfaced about what else may be found.

Now almost empty, the house took on a different perspective with assumptions abounding and feelings causing little heart skips. When all the rooms were empty and all the doors closed, G took one last look in the kitchen. As he slowly closed that door, there was a little clatter inside. He peered warily around to see a carrier bag hanging, which had knocked against the wood.

He took it off and carried it carefully to the trailer, fearing the worst. Should he look? Grenades maybe, another gun or diaries of a South London gangster? Oh no, more newspaper, not more chocolate.

It was quite heavy. On top of the trailer, newspapers were fearfully peeled away. It was something hard, round, grey and cold. Too big for a grenade; a helmet perhaps? No, it was a hibernating tortoise! So Uncle wasn't always so hard.

Orphan tortoise John, named after Uncle, is still in our garden sixteen years later. If he could talk, would he tell me about the guns and the suits? No, perhaps it is better to eat grass than to be one!

13 PUZZLES

How come the hair on my head and my eyebrows is greying when the hairs on my legs are still black?

How come my arms are getting longer whilst my sight is getting shorter?

Why can't I remember the next thing I was going to tell you?

Why is it when you are over forty, that it is either preferable to make love in the dark or to someone who can't see very well?

Or perhaps someone who doesn't really care too much?

Why because you trip over a couple of times and hurt yourself do your children think there is something wrong with your balance?

Why is it that a four-year-old grandchild thinks their grandparents are four-years-old, yet nine-year-old grandchildren are embarrassed by the antics of an oldie?

Why is it that parents don't think about their children's sex lives, but children think their parents don't have sex lives?

Why does it always rain after I have cleaned the windows?

Why are my laces further away when my backside is nearer the ground?

Why did my mother always sing so quietly to her grandchildren when she talked so loudly in public?

Why did the hair that disappeared so quickly from my dad's head reappear so rapidly through his ears and nose?

Why is it that the expensive and fashionable shoes worn by my son in his thirties are the same style as those he refused to wear when I was paying for them in his teens?

Why do people stay together when they are unhappy? Some time after the death of my husband a friend said, "I have been married for fifty years and we have nothing in common. We have come to terms with that. You on the other hand had so much in common, did and said everything. No regrets, eh?"

14 ROSEBUDS

I was thirty before I realised something was 'wrong'. Breasts weren't to the fore, no page three semi-nude models for everyone to see. Breasts were in books hidden from general view, in 'Men Only' magazines hidden under beds, in workshops, drawing offices and barber shops. Chauvinistic posters accompanied everyday sexism.

"Morning, Norma" said a voice from behind a drawing board. It took me ages to find out that this daily greeting was meant for Norma Snockers. This discovery being made after I had spent many weeks playing Miss Prissy and saying, "It's not Norma."

Norma – normal; I was not normal. Large, round, shapely breasts but with inverted nipples, a fact that was between me and perhaps a chosen few gentlemen who had managed to get beyond my 'boring Doreen'.

"Why did no one tell me?" I had two children who were denied breast feeding. At the time of their births I was made to feel inadequate, at one time being called "a dried up old cow". The maternity staff encountered then showed little TLC. I have since learned of nipple shields.

For years I felt lacking and different. In the sixties no one talked of breasts, let alone nipples.

Then the eighties arrived, there were bare breasts on the beaches, in the Sun and sometimes on TV! I knew no one who had inverted nipples; no one in the Sun had them! Not titillating to be bereft of proud nipples. So I kept the secret between me and my darling husband who accepted me as I was.

I have a friend and we worked closely for eleven years, remaining friends to the present day. One afternoon laughter turned to hysteria, as during a conversation, we simultaneously discovered each other had inverted nipples! Neither had known another similar person or had we? Just something no one talked about.

So I am not a freak of nature; there are at least two of us and although my nipples aren't proud, I am proud of them!

15 TEENAGERS IN THE FIFTIES

Life twists and turns and runs away with you, and you are old before a corner turns.

Teenagers in the fifties, what a different world; no television, Frankie Lane, Johnny Ray, skiffle groups with bases made from tea chests and string and highly strung drummers.

"What about Mantonvani and Tony Bennett?" Dad said as we played Paul Anka's *Diana* for the hundredth time until the hole in the middle of the seventy-eight grew bigger and distorted the sound.

Television came to our house, the first on our street. We stood nightly for the National Anthem; God blessed our Queen and I prayed to God. Church on Sunday, holy thoughts; school on Monday, naughty thoughts stirred by whispers and giggles about 'doing it'. What caused those tingles that came and went as I watched shirtless gardeners working in the beds at our all girls' school? Beds, was it something to do with beds?

Then came rock and roll; sin and the downfall of mankind. Whilst Lonnie was practising the nasty habit of placing used chewing gum on the bed frame, Bill Hayley was causing me to jump and jive and show my knickers and stocking tops. Not a pretty sight. Suspenders were attached to a corset, discreetly called a belt by my mother.

"Never go out without your belt, your stomach muscles will drop."

Now I was fat and I needed to flatten my stomach, but there were two consequences to wearing a corset.

Firstly, if you have a layer of extra body to flatten, it does not disappear by the use of such a painful device – it rises! It becomes another role of extra body around the waistline which has to be flattened by the use of another device called a long line bra. The next several hours are spent pulling one contraption up and the other down to ensure that the extra body does not escape and creep out of the middle to resemble a thick roll of pink plasticine.

The second and main consequence - these instruments of torture double as a chastity belt. My mother knew exactly what she was doing. If a young man ever managed to get through the barricade of top clothing, his passion immediately evaporated when touching solid wire-boned material, shuttering erogenous zones and divided by a roll of warm, pink putty spilling out of the middle. I was a very dutiful daughter, never went out without my belt, but rebelliously I never ever wore a vest!

Back to stocking tops; stockings were made for slim legs and were sized according to your shoes. Size five shoe plus fat legs – stockings reached just above the knee with suspenders dangling at the top of the thigh. The two could never meet. Fat girls with size five feet needed size seven stockings as these were longer and reached the suspenders. Longer, not wider, and the result was more of the pink flabby stuff bulging over the top of the stockings with indents from the suspenders. Why had no one invented tights?

In the fifties, women were objects of desire but not yet liberated. The majority of us were naïve men and women. There were youth clubs and groups, record players and seventy-eights. We were neither 'street' nor 'worldly' wise. Our world was that of cinema; Alan Ladd, 'Seven Brides for Seven Brothers', Kirk Douglas, Dick Barton, the Goons, the Archers and Billy Cotton. We had school biology lessons and were very knowledgeable about stamens and sepals and knew about frog reproduction. There were some hints about how babies were born, but how did they get there to enable them to be born?

A first kiss behind the side gate, terrified we might be seen. The fear was transmitted. I never saw him again but did, however, spend half the night dreaming of the kiss, my heart racing so fast I was sure Mum could hear it downstairs. My sweet mum found it so hard with teenage daughters. She had led a sheltered life, born in the early nineteen hundreds and in service from age fourteen to age thirty and then in service for my dear dad. She was embarrassed about 'the facts of life', and being positive that they had been covered at school, ensured that I remained ignorant, as did many of my friends. There had been some fumbling and mumblings at the back of the cinema, and a steady boyfriend was allowed a little exploration in the back of his car at Box Hill, but the fear of pregnancy and parental rejection ensured that actual sex before marriage was not an option.

Fifty years later friends and I discuss this sad state of affairs, so many young and inexperienced couples were true virgins on their wedding nights. The delight of sex learned in later years was overshadowed by the need to find a low rent bed sit and to make a date for the wedding to be carried out before the tax deadline of 6th April.

The night before my wedding mum asked if I wanted to know anything. Oh how much I wanted to say "yes". How terrified she was that I would do so, but I said "no". The result of this was two novice children searching for the right thing to do and say at the end of what should have been the happiest day in their lives.

I love the liberation started in the sixties and encouraged by Cosmo and TV. Sometimes I think we may have come too far, know too much and maybe we should compromise, but please never go back to the dark and secretive days without explanation.

16 NINE LIVES

You've heard of Murdock, lucky black cat? Sixteen years old, still going strong, still defending his territory, king of the road, on top of next door's conservatory looking out for predators. We were often at the vet, always tending his wounds.

"Don't be angry with him. He never runs away, his wounds are always on the front. Very brave cat," said the vet on what seemed to be our tenth visit in as many months.

"This has to be the most expensive cat anyone ever had," sighed my husband G. He would later regret this remark.

Murdi always wore a flea collar, bright red or bright blue against his jet black coat. Once I found him hanging from the fence where it had become caught; luckily we were at home. On another occasion he had been off his food for some days. We tried everything to coax him to eat; we cuddled him until he slept. On Saturday he didn't eat at all. That evening it was cold and raining sideways, the kind of night you stay in with a log fire and a warm cat on your lap, but Murdock wouldn't settle.

"I think his face is swollen," I said, "and he keeps pawing his ear". He cried out, obviously in pain. We tried hard to look in his mouth, but he would not let us near. Now I am very good when people are sick but hopeless with sick animals. Our vet was closed, either at home with his cat on his lap or spending an hour's wages at the Ritz.

I went into 'neurotic cat's mother' mode. We managed to find an emergency vet; so at 9 pm on this cold, wet night, we placed Murdock in his cat basket and drove to Tooting. I must have been really worried; I got my hair wet and didn't freak out.

As G carried him into the surgery, tears streamed down my cheeks and mixed with rain drops. I whispered, "If he has to be put to sleep, please let me be with him."

I expected to wait an age, but they were out in seconds with Murdi back in the basket. I gestured "What?" and looked at G's furious face.

"Take him to the car," he said whilst thrusting the keys at me.

I put the cat in the car and cooed a lot.

"You OK, darling?"

"Darling," a gruff voice bellowed behind me, "Who was the idiot who bought him a black collar?"

"What do you mean," I queried. His collar, black as has been noted, had worked loose. Instead of being round his neck, it was across his mouth like a tiny gag but still at the back of his neck! It couldn't be seen because of the black fur, and he had not allowed us to look in his mouth. He had been unable to move his jaw to eat but just enough to make pathetic cries.

"Sixty bloody pounds to remove a collar. What on earth possessed you to buy a black collar?"

"It was all they had" was my cringing and pathetic reply.

We sat in the car, soaked to the skin. I felt silly and I think my husband did too, but then the giggles began and we couldn't stop laughing.

"Let's take him home. He must be starving, aren't' you, mate? Live to fight another day, if your mother doesn't invent any more death traps for you."

17 THE MANAGER

How my children grew up to be managers of anything is beyond me; all are grown up now, some with children of their own. I have five small girls in my midst, produced from three large adults.

Being a grandmother is amazing. You can do all the things your grandchildren do and expect of you. It isn't until they are about five years old that they realise you are older than they are, so until that time, you get to skip, ride tricycles and sing all the Tweenies songs. After six years old you can still do these things, and they laugh calling you 'crazy Nanny'. Above eight years they become very self-conscious and beg you not to embarrass them.

"People are looking, Nan."

Anyway, back to the manager.

From time to time these girlies need some discipline, to toe the line or get in line. I am neither an ogre, nor a disciplinarian and I believe that with them, as with my own children, love guides and directs.

However, at the times when a little more was needed, I called upon **'The Manager'**.

This faceless person is everywhere, on trains, in public lavatories, fast food places, retail stores, theme parks. One tantrum, or 'strop' to use a modern term, is quashed by a swift look into the distance and a firm, "Quick, the Manager is coming."

It worked with my boys, works every time with the girlies. I tried it last week in the WCQ at St James's Park when my youngest girlie would not come inside with me. At the mention of 'the Manager', she shot in and stood by my side.

The woman behind me smiled and said, "Don't we threaten with a policeman any more?"

18 SAS

One Sunday morning, my sons were getting a little bored. It was too wet to go out and before the days of computer games. "I'll make them laugh," I thought.

I ran quietly upstairs, donned a pair of tights on my head and pulled one leg over my face, squashing my features into a flat American tan nightmare. I found a toy gun, crept downstairs, got on to the floor on my belly and crawled, commando-style into the lounge.

Both boys looked up; at first startled, then the older one's face broke into a smile. Not so the younger, he jumped onto the sofa, screaming at the top of his voice and when I realised his fear, I pulled off my mask and threw down my weapon.

This did not work!

He continued to shout, scream and jump up and down. I grabbed his shoulder, shouting into his face, "I am your mother for goodness sake. It was just a joke."

Ten minutes later he calmed down. He didn't forgive me for weeks and has grown up into a really stable man – no thanks to me!

19 TURKISH DELIGHT

We finished our short course in car mechanics, and you know I could repair anything provided the engine was out of its housing and up on a bench! Friends laughed at us, two women auto-mechanics; this was the early eighties. They laughed even more when the car broke down and we had to call out the AA on the way home from the first lesson.

So we thought perhaps something more feminine for next term.

"How about belly dancing?" J said. This was to be held at the same venue as car mechanics but in the hall, not the workshop. I spent half-term making the costume; this was an achievement for me. I covered a flesh pink bra with green sequins and added tassels and bells.

We were all shapes and sizes, ages and abilities. J looked fantastic; the twenty years difference in our ages was obvious, my 'belly' having borne two children. We cavorted, tripped, danced and wobbled around the room, prostrating ourselves on the wooden floor, which no one had cleaned since the boys left at 4 pm. The smell of the dust penetrated our nostrils as it was stirred up by the bare and slowly blackening feet.

After a few weeks we were fed up with going home both tired and even dirtier than we had been from the mechanics class, so we all agreed to pay a little extra and go to the teacher's dance studio. This prospect was quite exciting. A real studio, we must be good.

Well, it is easy to prance around a hall as you watch classmates swivel their knees and jelly their bellies, but when we saw ourselves mirrored in the studio walls, it was not only hysterical but unbelievable. We became so embarrassed and self-conscious that it took another six weeks to reach the standard at which we had left the boys' school. However, being an extrovert and an exhibitionist, I soon began to enjoy wiggling without giggling.

After a while I was commissioned to do two performances at the fortieth and fiftieth birthdays of two friends' husbands. I was to awaken them on their birthday morn by dancing at the bottom of their beds and presenting them with a tray of Turkish Delight, surprising them but with the full consent of their spouses. The first performance went smoothly.

The second show was at 7 am on a cold February morning. I knocked gently on the front door for his wife to let me in, but no one came. Ten minutes passed. My youngest son, oblivious of the plan, walked past the house with his bag of newspapers and was suddenly confronted by his shivering mum wearing very little. This twelve-year-old has never forgiven me. The second twelve-year-old to be embarrassed was the son of the house who opened the door to be greeted by green sequined shivering boobs.

"Mum, Mrs. B is here and she has no clothes on."

My friend, hearing the shout, almost fell down the stairs and rushed me into the house.

Some few minutes elapsed before I was warm enough to turn my shivers into seductive gyrations.

The performance eventually went well, but the episode affected the boys. My son wouldn't talk to me for days. The other lad, moved in a different way, often asked when I would be wearing the outfit again!

20 HANDS ACROSS THE SEA

Americans and other ex pats for that matter had a difficult time in London in the eighties. Eating was a particular pastime and important if you were away from home. But all restaurants were closed on a Sunday, except perhaps for the newly opened McDonalds and very expensive hotels.

"Would you like to come to lunch?" I asked Wayne Spencer III, a young Texan on his own. We opened our home to many visitors from time to time as a gesture of hospitality but also to broaden our minds. We offered a traditional English roast and all the trimmings, sprouts being particularly popular with Italians!

Unfortunately not all of our neighbours were as broadminded and felt it their God given right to know the full itinerary of the week in the house of a divorcee with two sons.

I hate net curtains – nothing to hide, nothing to peer from behind.

The taxi stopped.

"Oh for goodness sake, he is going next door!" I couldn't go out and rescue him from the Witch of the West, so she took great pleasure in redirecting him. When he eventually arrived and courtesies were over, we sat at the table in the window and started lunch.

Mid conversation I glanced outside where there seemed to be more activity than usual, especially as there was a typical London drizzle in the air.

"Is that Dennis walking the dog and Sarah too?" Our neighbour from across the road was so concentrating on peering through my window that he caught his leg in the dog lead and fell face down into my hedge. Sarah did her best to extricate him, at the same time calming and untangling the dog.

To my horror I realised that the passing traffic embraced a succession of neighbours either walking their dogs or taking an unusual Sunday stroll with their heads turned left or right. Dennis emerged from the hedge and was replaced by Peter, who was followed by Pat.

Eventually the rain and the traffic stopped. Wayne left.

The next day Mrs. G stopped me. "Saw your friend dear, young wasn't he? Long hair, glasses and a very expensive coat, foreign is he? Shall we see him again soon?"

Oh suburbia, nosey suburbia. My next visitor, whom she didn't see, came through the back door in the dark when I was alone.

21 HARD HAT

I'm not old, but have needed the use of diuretics since my mid thirties. Just once a day mind, but they necessitate careful planning of the enfolding day to accommodate an hour of "peeing like 50,000 boy scouts" as one old friend so delicately described it to me.

We were travelling to a conference on the Herts border. Just a few more miles and we would be there in time for breakfast.

"If I take it now, the peak would be over by the 10 am start." So down it went with a large swallow of water.

I sat back, listened to 'Magic', closed my eyes and drifted with the Drifters.

"Why have we stopped, love?"

"Road works" was the reply.

I disappeared again to a California beach. "Oh, wouldn't it be nice" the boys sang to me.

"Why aren't we moving?"

"There must have been an accident."

The songs came and went, the cars didn't. The travel news told us of an accident just a little north of where we sat. Time passed, we moved slowly, slowly matching the sips from the water bottle edging slowly, slowly down, down, down. The diesel tank emptied, my bladder filled.

A break in the jam and we started to move, not at speed but moving.

"I shall need to wee soon."

"For God's sake, we've only just started to move." He sounded gruff but was truly sympathetic to my needs having lived with me for seventeen years, travelling the world seeking lavatories! We were lavatorial experts ranging from one foot on each side of a hole in Lagos to buying a very small but expensive amount of toilet paper in Rome.

"I really must go soon, darling."

My bladder was stretched to its limits and the discomfort increasing.

"I really need to go soon," my high pitched voice squeaked in desperation.

"Look, there, just off the road. McDonalds. We could use the toilet and get you some coffee."

No sooner said than we ground to a halt again, inching forward almost motionless.

"Ferry cross the Mersey," spouted Gerry.

"Please," I thought, "Please don't remind me of water."

I released my seat belt and got up on my knees facing the rear, but the pain was unrelenting and my bladder almost bursting.

Slowly moving, we eventually turned left into the industrial estate and screeched to a halt outside the fast food place. I rushed to the door, it was locked. The staff were busy inside.

"What time is it?"

"Six forty-five and they don't open until seven am."

I hammered on the door and they ignored me. I began to cry, doubled in agony. My husband rushed to the door gesticulating and shouting. He was greeted by gestures to wrist watches and looks of disgust. I cried out in pain whilst he looked in vain for somewhere, comforting me with his arm.

We had a huge Volvo estate. He lifted the hatch.

"Climb in."

"What?" I questioned.

"Climb in," he shouted again. The climb increased the pressure on my bladder.

Do you remember sun ray pleated skirts? I had a black one.

"Squat," he ordered.

"What?"

"Squat – here. No one will see you."

My hero, my saviour, my inventive engineer discreetly turned his back and handed me the safety helmet kept for site visits. I peed a torrent I thought would never stop and possibly flow over on to the boot carpet. The relief was etched on my face by a smile that broadened and did not give a clue as to the slight smell of acetone creeping from under the black tent which covered my plight.

Equally discreetly my husband removed the receptacle and deposited the contents into a nearby drain. Returning to the car he helped me to alight with grace and ease, compose myself and return to the passenger seat to continue the journey. As he used the remainder of the water bottle to flush out the inside of the hat, McDonalds opened their doors for the first coffees of the day!

He never used the hat again, but it remained in the boot for possible future emergencies.

22 GANGSTER 'WRAPPER'?

My niece came out of a London station at one o'clock in the morning with her friend. They were sharing the earphones of her personal CD player. They were bobbing in unison and watching the breath from their giggles float off into the night air. It was quiet with no sign of sleepers and snorers in tenement bed-sits. A little hint of dissipating two-stroke oil lingered in the wake of a long gone 950-cc motor bike, and there could have been engine noise in the far distance. No birds; no early morning traders; no paper sellers – all yet to wake.

They didn't notice him initially, but suddenly there he was standing right in front of them, barring their way, halting their dancing, freezing their laughter.

He was tall, black and with a gleaming smile. He wore a long black coat, plus a trilby hat that topped his shaved head and was pulled down over one eye. He later told them this had cost him fifty pence at the charity shop. He tugged at the yellow cravat warming his neck. A small gun-shaped earring swung gently from one ear.

"Hello ladies. Can I escort you home?"

As he drew nearer they saw he had a heavy beard. As his head turned a little, the light caught words shaved into it. On the right cheek, 'Hot' and on the left, 'Sex'.

The two girls moved closer to each other, both fearful, neither speaking. His voice was deep, his stature large. There was no one else to be seen in the area. They turned to walk a little quicker towards their home, and he fell in step beside them.

"Truly, ladies, I will keep you safe from harm. London is not a place for young unescorted women in the early hours. I am part of the neighbourhood safety squad and will see you safely to your door."

They could not force him away. If they ran, he could outrun them. His huge hands could knock them to the ground; they would both be overpowered in seconds. "Did he have a knife? Did he carry a gun?" The thoughts made them shiver.

Noticing this he put his huge arm around her shoulder. The fear inside almost overwhelmed her and she wanted to break into flight.

He jabbered on about his role in the London night, and they seemed to be walking but not moving. His huge presence seemed to be part of the dark night, enveloping them.

Suddenly he stopped; looking her straight in the eye he grabbed hold of her CD player as if to steal it and run off. She was almost relieved and wished he would go now. The player was tiny in his great hands and he could have crushed it in one movement.

He pulled away, stopped, turned and raised his arm as if he was about to strike. Was this the moment; were they about to experience the terror they felt inside?

"Have you got any Chris de Burgh?"

23 ROOKIE

The year 1963; we were all in our early twenties, and by today's mature standards, going on fifteen. We went to the Isle of Wight for the weekend and after a late fish and chip supper, walked on the beach. There was an open beach hut so we all decided to go skinny dipping, something almost unheard of then, especially in the Isle of Wight.

We laughed a lot, and although some of us were bold enough to remove all our clothes, one or two stopped at the BHS underwear. The water was so cold that extremities either shrivelled or protruded depending on gender. We splashed, swam, dived, shouted, screamed and lost all sense of time and the hour. We ran back to the hut, hugging each other for warmth and hoping we would be dry enough to put back our clothes. Shivers caused giggles and these turned to laughter. Horseplay continued with the echoes of screaming into the night.

Suddenly, flashes of light outside combined with loud voices.

"Come out of there, this is the police." Our shivers froze as did our laughter. Hurriedly, we tried to put on clothes that stuck to clammy sandy skin. "Come out now!"

"Christ," he whispered, "I can't be arrested." This was an obvious statement as he was in the middle weekend of his training course with the Metropolitan Police at Hendon.

"Come out now or we'll come in there."

"We must save him," she said, "Take off your clothes."

"What?"

"Take them off. If we go out naked, they might be distracted and we can cover him with all our clothes."

Seven of us crept out on to the sand with our bits and pieces moving with fright and cold. Two very young PCs moving their flashlights from body to body.

"What do we have here then, an orgy in South West England?"

"Sorry officers, we were swimming and got carried away. I apologise if we made so much noise. We are on holiday and the bright moonlight and warmth caused us to forget the time."

My friend was brilliant. She had stood in front of the young PC, endeavouring to look him straight in the eye, but his eyes were elsewhere.

"By rights, Miss, we should arrest you for being drunk and disorderly."

"But officer, I promise it won't happen again, we will go home now."

She turned slightly, enough to pose provocatively with the moonlight shimmering on her ample silhouette. Both PCs took a step forward, hands on belts, torches shuddering slightly. It seemed an age before they spoke.

"OK then, you are let off this time, but don't let us find you here again. Go on, get dressed."

They turned and walked back to the steps. We all dashed back into the hut, dressing quickly.

"Where is she?"

I peeked outside to see my extrovert friend at the top of the steps, alabaster in the moonlight, waving to two policemen on bikes riding off into the distance.

She ran back to us. "They've gone now, they'll never know there were eight of us." Saying this she grabbed her things and ran off along the beach, twirling her knickers above her head.

One career saved.

24 CORFU

What a beautiful island with mountains, green and lush, a bit like Wales with sun; then the wonderful coves with a brilliant blue sea edged by sandy crescents and honey for sale at every bend on the mountain roads. There were fake tee shirts, the odd goat and dark-skinned grey-haired men, some with and some without teeth. We hired a car for the day to go up into the mountains.

We had heard about a deserted village. When we arrived, it was not quite deserted, as there was a tea room! We had a coffee, said goodbye to fellow travellers and made our way along a track that disappeared into trees. We had been told there was a road over the mountains.

"Are you sure about this?" I asked my husband, "Doesn't seem like a road."

"Stop whining," he replied, revving harder as the dirt road became steeper. The smell of the dry earth seeped through the open windows, and the tyres blew little clouds of dust in front and behind the car. We were almost to the point where the road became indistinguishable from the trees, and although I was unable to recognise them, the smell was wonderful as we were shaded from the morning sun.

Suddenly as he changed down a gear and the car struggled to keep momentum, a tall menacing looking man stepped out of the bushes. He was carrying a large rifle and had a bandolier of bullets across his chest. He raised his hand, we had to stop.

"Turn round, turn round for God's sake, it's a bloody bandit."

"But I want to go over the mountain," he said, still revving the engine.

The man had now been joined by an equally fierce looking woman in dark and dirty clothes, wearing a beret. She was shaking her head and hitting her knees.

"Either she wants us to walk or she is saying she will kneecap us if we get out of the car. For heaven's sake, please turn round."

The man started to raise his rifle and aimed it at the windscreen. My partner could then see the sense of reversing and tearing back down the mountain. He had been a racing car driver many years before and used the handbrake to change direction with one manoeuvre. We sent up a huge cloud of dust that obscured the man's vision and sped to safety at about fifty miles an hour.

Bandits on Corfu, never.

25 MUSIC (1)

Before TV, there was wireless. I am old enough to have been brought up without television and to remember 'Friday Night is Music Night', Radio Luxembourg and Billy Cotton's Band show.

My Dad had been a musician in the army and often sat on the settee next to his record player, conducting military bands. I am still stirred by the sounds accompanying the Changing of the Guard and the Salvation Army in our High Street at Christmas. I can also pick out the euphonium in all brass band tunes.

Music is in my heart and my soul. From early years I sang, not always in the bath, as initially this was the tin type in front of the fire once a week because 'Friday night was also bath night'. Our next home was a two up, two down council house with a bathroom, but again I could not sing in the bath as I had to share this with my sister before Mum and Dad took turns. I realise now this was because we could not afford to heat more than one bath full of water.

As we grew older my sister and I did duets and 'shows' for very patient relatives. In my teens I became part of the church choir and the special twelve voice choir at school. Sadly there was nowhere to practice at home; everything had to be done in the front room. This was the only room, and in the winter we all stayed there as the gas fire was the main source of heating. We sometimes lit the oven in the kitchen whilst we had a quick wash and cleaned our teeth. The bedrooms were always freezing, and often on a winter's morning, the net curtains had become stuck to the windows where condensation had turned into ice.

Getting ready for bed we undressed in front of the gas fire, shivered in the lavatory, then raced to jump under the blankets and flannelette sheets to cuddle our hot water bottles. When I awoke my nose and ears were always cold.

Suffice to say the bedroom was too cold to stand and sing, and the radio was always on in the front room. Where could I sing?

I often wonder now if the neighbours could hear me. I sat in the upstairs lavatory with my coat on, and although my family still remember this with a smile or a laugh, in my mind I was at the Albert Hall singing my wonderful rendition of 'One Fine Day' and 'Oh my beloved father'.

With neither the money nor the knowledge to encourage me further than the church and school choirs, I became a shrinking violet and did not sing again 'in public' until the age of fifty.

26 TELEVISION

I had an aunt who lived in central London and shopped in Harvey Nicholls. She spent many weekends with us. Our home was inviting and loving and my mum was a wonderful cook. One weekend in the fifties, my aunt brought a small black and white television set and left it with us so we could watch it during the week. It was fascinating, but there were often breakdowns in transmission and broadcasts were interspersed with 'the interlude'.

My favourite was the 'Potter's Wheel'. We were enthralled by a wonderful pot being thrown but never finished. My dad loved the steam train which was shown at great speed going from London to the south coast. There was also a shaded test card which enabled the contrast to be adjusted.

The broadcast time was not very long and every evening ended with 'the epilogue' and the National Anthem, for which we all stood.

I can remember Muffin the Mule, but very little else as I was still very attached to the wireless.

We did, however, become the most popular family in our street when 'cup ties' were shown on Saturday afternoons.

27 MUSIC (II)

I had a demanding job that I loved, but sadly, brought it home a lot.

"You're boring me to death; talk about something else for goodness sake."

This remark from my husband prompted me to research the library to find a hobby that would take my mind off work. Singing, could I sing again? I hadn't sung for thirty-two years except for lullabies, nursery rhymes and pop songs.

'The DC Singers' it read, 'concerts for charity'. I called the number. They met on Monday not far from my home. There was no audition, just a little probation and the most important answer to my questioning was that they did not have to make their own costumes!

I went along to a rehearsal and joined in the songs, sitting in the back row. I really had a fantastic time and couldn't wait for the next Monday. I found it so difficult to sleep as the songs were buzzing in my head.

"It seems funny sitting on seats and singing," I remarked to my man.

"For goodness sake, go to sleep," he barked.

The third week I volunteered to set out the chairs.

"No chairs this week, we are starting the movement."

"Movement?" I questioned.

"Well, dancing really."

"Oh no, I can't dance," I exclaimed, panic setting in. I must add here that I was five feet two inches, size sixteen and did not own a sports bra. I am not sure if there were sports bras then.

"Of course you can, if you can sing, you can dance."

We did two public shows each year and took them to homes, hospitals and anywhere else we were asked or where there was a captive audience!

The size sixteen mentioned above brought with it a built in fear of communal changing rooms, self-conscious awareness of the extra load being carried in the area of my waist. When did I last have a waist? My thighs left a lot to be desired. 'Desire' is not a word that should be in the same sentence as 'my thighs'.

We rehearsed for weeks, we giggled and sweated. Our director and the producers were brilliant and very patient. I stayed at the back and enjoyed myself but then came the dress rehearsal. We had a cupboard at each side of the stage for girls and boys. The pain of seventeen returned as I had to reveal the relationship between me and my undies, but there was no time for embarrassment as we were in and out of costumes in seconds. I became a little bolder with each change.

The opening night, my stomach was churning. I hadn't eaten all day and the more experienced members were very supportive.

"Have a little drink to steady your nerves." I didn't drink but took a few sips. My heart began to pound and as I followed the chorus from the side to centre stage, I felt my heart pounding so fast I was sure I was going to die there and then. Suddenly I realised I liked it. I was an extrovert, a show off. I really liked it. A star was born, well, a twinkle anyway.

When the show was over, we visited places where changing rooms were cupboards or offices, boys and girls together. Again speed overcame shyness. We did many repeat performances, often visiting twice a year. People anticipated our shows. At one home we had to change behind a curtain. I arrived a little late, carrying my costumes and was almost crushed by two elderly men in wheelchairs racing along the corridor.

"Sorry, darlin', we're going to see the girls!"

Now these 'girls' ranged from forty to sixty-five, but I suppose if you are into your eighties, possibly with only memories left and failing sight, a flash of a bra strap and fishnets going on or coming off can be quite erotic.

We sang and danced on stages, in halls, in canteens and in rooms the size of my lounge. We were versatile, learning all the parts in case someone was sick. We learned to keep singing in spite of ammonia smells and kept dancing around chair and table legs. At one venue we all danced very close together, bunched at one end of the room, endeavouring to avoid deposits left earlier at the other end.

We smiled and sang louder when someone in the audience shouted, "nurse, nurse" or "You sang that just now". We continued to smile as an old man navigated our prancing ranks shouting, "I'm just going to get me tablets."

Many residents loved our performances and often joined in our songs, but there were others who had been forced to sit and watch. One old man deliberately stuck out his legs, trying really hard to trip us as we danced past him.

This hobby enhanced my life, helped me fulfil a long held ambition to sing and stopped me from boring my husband. He may have lived to regret his remark a little, as I was often out three times each week and every weekend.

Be very careful what you wish for.

28 SIN BIN

In the late fifties a great uproar was caused by the publication of *Lady Chatterley's Lover*. The book was subsequently banned. It contained what was then considered to be too explicit sex scenes and swearing. Working in the centre of London I was able to borrow a copy from a friend. The book is really tame by today's standards.

I used to read this at night, but kept it in a cover of *Great Expectations*, hoping Mum would not notice.

I was not as anxious or inventive as a friend of mine who read it secretly, but put it in the dustbin before she went to bed in case she died during the night!

29 WALLS HAVE EARS

My mum loved her net curtains, just the right thickness to keep her privacy but enough to allow her to see out. She knew everything that went on, but never anyone's name, so she invented them. Mr. and Mrs. Postman, Mrs. Welsh Woman, Old Blue Suit, the Bookie and the Cleaner Girls.

I related this recently to a friend who said, "We call our neighbours Mr. and Mrs. O because of the noise that frequently comes through the adjoining bedroom walls." It seems this couple were so active it affected their neighbours' sleep pattern. My friend found it hard not to blush the morning after when prim and proper Mrs. O waved over the fence as they both started out for work.

Mr. and Mrs. O went on holiday and left the key with my friend to feed the cats and generally keep an eye on the place. On the last night before the O's return from holiday, my friend visited her neighbours' bedroom and pulled the bed away from the wall, just enough not to notice but hopefully prevent further sleepless nights on the other side of the cavity.

They are unsure if this was ever detected but were told recently by Mrs. O that she had redecorated her bedroom and "turned the room around".

My friend is now sleeping better; not sure about the people on the other side though!

30 MASS HYSTERIA

I went to the pictures (cinema/movies) in the late fifties with my sister and her friend.

"You must come, he's wonderful," she said.

We saw Elvis Presley in *Jailhouse Rock*. All the girls were screaming, jumping out of their seats, pulling their clothes and each other and some of them crying. I screamed and screamed along with the crowd.

Suddenly I stopped, realising I really didn't like Elvis that much. I sat for the remainder of the film, no one noticing, and I couldn't hear anything.

Some time later I went with my church to Wembley. Billy Graham was preaching and imploring people to "Come down and be saved". His voice was so powerful. Many were moved, so much so that a sea of people was falling like a torrent down the steps and in front of their saviour.

"Come, come," he entreated. Without warning I found myself pulled from my seat by some unknown force, a child swept along by the frenzy and going to meet God.

Halfway down I was awakened.

"I've already been saved," I said, remembering that I had been confirmed some two months past. "Where to now?" I thought, "I can't go back." A quick dart to the left and I was seated again.

Some five years later and an adult, supposedly, the Beatles were at Wimbledon Palais, long since demolished and replaced by furniture stores and now homes. I liked their music so I thought I would go. So did thousands of others, screaming and shouting to their idols. I got pushed further and further back and neither saw nor heard them, but I didn't scream either.

31 DOLLY?

A fortieth birthday party, a fancy dress; my husband groaned and dug his heels in saying reluctantly he would go but definitely not dress up. I was sixty, uninhibited and willing to play the game. I bought a Dolly Parton wig, denim jacket, revealing top and a *Wonderbra!*

I pulled on my jeans and boots, moulded my ample breasts into the bra and inserted the magic pads that enabled them to 'praise the Lord' in good old country style. I then slipped into the top from which they almost escaped. I added the jacket and the blonde wig – big wig! I then sprayed this with glitter and finally attached six inch pendants to each ear. All the aforementioned items had to be in place before I applied my very thick and bright make up and inch long false nails, the latter being painted with vivid red polish to match the big bright voluptuous orifice beneath my nose. All done, I sat for ten minutes to ensure that nothing would either smudge or move.

I walked slowly, gingerly down the stairs calling in my best Southern accent.

"Ahm ready, honey."

Honey was at the bottom of the stairs with his camera poised; I wished I had been holding it to capture the look on his face.

"Do you expect me to go out with you looking like that? We could be arrested."

He would not even walk to the car with me, but had to wait to open the door as I could neither touch nor carry a thing and had to slide very carefully into the seat to ensure nothing was dislodged. Grudgingly he fastened my seat belt.

At the party I was a wow, everyone was amazed at the transformation. My daughter-in-law, who wore a wonderful animal skin number topped by a long blonde wig, loudly commented that she never thought she would be 'out blonded' by her mother-in-law. My grandchildren were fascinated how my nails could have grown so long in the twenty-four hours since we had been together. The four-year-old was anxious to ensure that I would be able to get my real hair back soon.

It was my sister, however, who was the most curious and intrigued, slowly studying from head to toe. After a few minutes she asked, "Where did you get those boobs? You didn't have them last week."

"Oh yes, I did," was my reply, "But they were three inches lower!"

32 WATER AEROBICS

I had been very active in my middle age years; I danced, walked and rode a bike. We often cycled forty miles on a Saturday. I planned that on retiring, I was going to build on these activities to keep fit and fill my spare time. I joined a local 'twirlies' group and three times a week I tried line, tap and jazz dancing and carried on cycling. I was fit and happy. Two weeks into this regime, I fell down a step and tore ligaments in my leg and tendons in my foot. This put an end to any exercise for at least a year.

After that year I was desperate to return to a fitness programme, but on GP's advice, this had to be nonweight bearing. Something water-based was what we agreed upon. The next Wednesday morning at the local pool I started water aerobics. The music was loud, the teacher fit, slim and young. An assortment of students, all over fifty-five, wearing an array of swimwear, stood in the water beside floats of various shapes and colours. Multicoloured skins either gained at birth or during a quick visit to the adjacent sun beds were topped with multicoloured hair. The exercise started by bobbing up and down and 'Eureka', the water displacement was phenomenal!

Now I am about five feet two inches; the shallowest water was four feet. I stayed at the front to enable me to see and hear as both of these senses had faded somewhat in recent years. I jumped in time with the beat, raising my legs as instructed, a couple of time slipping on the greasy bottom. This resulted in my flailing about, coughing and spitting, attempting to regain my balance and keep my dignity. I was told much later that it was preferable to wear socks when dancing in water.

The rhythm continued as we hopped and swayed; raising arms above heads caused me to slip again and repeat my underwater floundering. Whilst trying to regain my composure and my position, I caught sight of the woman beside me endeavouring to avoid a single drop of water from reaching anywhere above her shoulders. She had full and thick makeup, hair held up with a chiffon scarf and huge pendant earrings swaying every which way. Her chin was pointed almost to the balcony as she screwed up her nose and eyes avoiding the impending droplets. She too should have been told about the use of socks before she disappeared backwards, feet up, head down.

The speed of the music increased as did the height of the leaps. Now I was well away. At every bound the water cushioned the impact on my knees and other joints. There was, however, no cushioning for the upper body; my breasts flying northward on the upward leap and pounding on the water on the way south. At the break I made my way a little deeper to enable my breasts to stay under water. The waves from the surrounding overweight seniors knocked me sideways and filled my nose with spray.

We finished, and following a shower, I made my way home clutching my bosom which was sore beyond belief. After trying all kinds of shuttering, none of which could be worn under a 'cosie', I decided to research less sadistic forms of exercise.

33 LINE DANCE

Music is my first love, dancing my second. When you are over sixty, people expect decorum; maybe a spot of ballroom dancing with the odd Tuesday afternoon tea dance, perhaps? I don't feel over sixty and have never practised anything remotely decorous.

I decided to do a bit of line dancing, which was absolutely wonderful. Although not a particular country music fan, I was able after a few sessions to enjoy the music, pick up the beat and fit in the steps. The majority of my fellow dancers were over forty. One of them was over eighty, so although the dances kept us fit, nothing was too onerous. Line dancing involves some very intricate foot work but little upper body movement; it is necessary, however, to keep complete concentration or else you can find yourself facing the wrong wall in a 'four wall' sequence, at the same time as staring into the eyes of the oncoming dancers. The other necessity is a bottle of water to be sipped or gulped when the music stops.

When I saw a class in Latin American line dancing, I felt I could progress to this. My experiences of a fruit topped Carmen Miranda from the cinema of my childhood, combined with Edmundo Ross of the fifties and the modern day Ricky Martin and Gloria Estefan, had given me the confidence to cha cha cha behind closed doors. Surely I could transfer these skills to the local Adult Institute?

The only similarity to my experience of line dancing was the word line! The class was bigger, average age younger and the music much faster. I loved the music and was able to keep to the beat; dancing is dancing is dancing. What I did not account for was the huge increase in my heartbeat and energy output. I would surely need a larger bottle of water. One hour and fifteen minutes of pure Latin dance without a break caused my body to sweat and me to realise that my clothes were far too thick. Another amazing discovery of the difference between the two forms of dance is that the Latin type calls for great upper body movement and quite a bit of high stepping. These two, combined with a thirty-eight D cup M & S bra, caused bouncing similar to that experienced in the swimming pool, except that there was nothing to cushion either the north or south movements.

I am determined to succeed. It is a wonderful form of exercise, but last week I took part wearing light leggings, a cotton top and a heavy duty sports bra. Gloria Estefan or Carmen Miranda I was not, but I was able to get through the evening with the whole of my upper body swaying to the beat and not going off in a completely uncontrolled direction.

34 I DO

We had been together for eleven years, and he felt it good to affirm our love by marrying; I did not feel the need but agreed because I loved him. We had a wonderful celebration with special family and friends; it was a happy, happy time.

We have always loved the Thames and he booked a hotel where this wonderful river tumbled down a weir. Our room overlooked this spectacle, and the sound was both soothing and enjoyable. The very famous place had a world-wide reputation both for location and sumptuousness and the price reflected this.

We had only one night away, so it had to be very special. He arranged for beautiful flowers in our room, and as I am a teetotal vegetarian, requested a bowl of my favourite fruit. The room was typically English with a blue theme; the view from our window was magnificent. As were the flowers, but no fruit. He phoned reception and also spoke to the staff to ensure it would be there when we returned from our riverside stroll. We had been friends and lovers all our life together and walking hand in hand we laughed and talked, remembering the lovely day that was fading fast.

On arrival back at our room we discovered that nothing had changed, the environment not augmented by a bowl of fruit. He called reception again this time with a little edge to his voice. We toasted each other with coffee and juice and prepared ourselves to experience the towelling robes, monogrammed slippers and very expensive bed linen.

Still no one came. I told him not to worry; I would eat fruit in the morning. It was now nearly ten o'clock and although consummation was not a word to use after so many years of practise, we began to celebrate the first night as a married couple.

Passion, temperatures and joy rising, we started as we would have done as young marrieds, but with more experience of life and each other, knowing what pleased.

"What the ….?"

"There's someone at the door," I answered.

"Go away," he shouted.

"Room service." The reply came in a very strong East European accent.

"Go away, we are sleeping."

Knocking again, the young man called "Room Service" a little louder.

By the third knock which was fast becoming hammering, my husband, his passion abating and his temper rising angrily shouted, "Just a moment."

He rose from the bed, grabbed his gown just as the door flew open; the young man, not understanding, had used his pass key.

He stood astounded in the doorway, proffering a fruit bowl to the nude and equally astounded middle aged newlyweds.

In the morning my husband complained bitterly to the manager, who asked us to take breakfast whilst he investigated.

As we ate, we laughed at our experience, seeing the humour in the situation until we received the bill which included extra charges for breakfast and a bowl of fruit!

35 CONDITIONING

There is a Welsh saying 'It's the way your mam put your hat on'. This covers all the idiosyncratic, possibly weird things we do in our lives, things which were programmed in our youth; superstitions, fears, inexplicable terrors and phobias.

How many people will not put new shoes on the table; not open an umbrella indoors; throw spilled salt over their shoulders? Which shoulder should it be anyway? There are very common phobias of spiders, stepping on pavement cracks, seeing the new moon through glass, but a fear of cooling towers?

Journeys north either meant a detour if driving or with eyes closed as a passenger in order to avoid viewing those towers in the vicinity of Birmingham. My partner was not at all understanding of what he considered my irrational behaviour.

Obviously if I had lived near to the towers, the phobia would have been a bigger problem, but working in the area of mental health, I felt it part of my personal development to analyse and rationalise such gremlins; part of this analysis included a family discussion. I talked at length to my elderly father, my dear mother having died. At this time we discovered that Dad had always suffered from a fear of tall buildings which included pylons and cooling towers. This fear had either been subconsciously transmitted or associated as a child.

At this discovery I was able to realise that this fear was not mine and although not 'in love' with these giant edifices, I could now concentrate on my fear of ants!

36 REMEMBER, REMEMBER

Last night I watched fireworks through a window; much safer. The noises start with the odd one set off by naughty boys at about three forty-five in the afternoon in the middle of October. This progresses to displays on or about Halloween and continue well past Guy Fawkes' night. There are fantastic shows of pyrotechnic achievements at the midnight herald of a new year and Disney has them all over the world at the end of another fantasy filled day.

Fireworks bigger, brighter, more colourful and often accompanied by booms of thunder, shaking the foundations of our homes, but frequently bringing injury and death; does no one listen to the warnings?

Warnings? I was a war baby and the flood warning siren sometimes used on the Thames causes the hairs on the back of my neck to rise. I was born in Camberwell; Mum told me we were bombed twice before we went to Lancashire. The second bomb went through my pram; obviously as this writing testifies, I was somewhere else at the time!

Bonfire night we called it. We had a large bonfire and a small box of Woolworth fireworks; Golden Rain, Roman Candle, Catherine Wheel, Sparklers and a Banger. I hated them all and still do, but those that frightened me the most were Jumpin Jax as they zigzagged all around the garden making an awful cracking noise. They must have been really tame compared with today's explosive nightmares. I recall Dad affixed Catherine Wheels to our fence by means of a pin!

All of the bonfires thickened the polluting smog caused by coal smoking chimneys. The smell of sulphur crept from the nose to the throat, initiating little coughs or aggravating bronchial chests

The best parts of the fifth of November were the following supper of chip butties and the thought that the next celebration, just a few weeks away, would be Christmas.

37 T' MILL

I was too small to remember the journey from Camberwell to Todmorden, but it must have been by steam train. In the crevices that hold memories, I can see pictures of my aunt's café above which, I think, we must have lived. Can't ask them now, they're all gone, mum, dad, aunt and uncle and perhaps also the men in dungarees and clogs, the women in pinafores and turbans with different coloured protruding 'bangs'.

They worked in the mills and came for their dinners served in the middle of the day. They sat in high-backed booths, smoked Woodbines and drank tea sweetened with saccharine and served in enamel mugs. The mugs had turned over rims, sometimes with little black chips on the edges; no one fussed, the tea was good and this was 'the War'. There was a mixture of smells, sometimes people, often fags and always the warm inviting aroma of meat and potato pies covered in homemade crusty pastry made with lard. Where on earth did they get the meat from; what about rationing? Did they bring their coupons? The inside window, which was opaque at the bottom, steamed up when it rained outside.

It rained a lot in Todmorden, the park opposite testifying to this by the full trees and grassy green slopes edging the steep path to the bottom of the hill. My cousin was ten years older than me and offered each day to take me for a walk in the pram. This was a welcome break for mum as she was the 'washer up' at dinner time. After a while she became suspicious; leaving the café and lighting her Woodbine, she followed him at a distance when she suddenly saw him jump on to the chassis of the pram and holding on to the handle, move at great speed down the hill, the sleeping bairn oblivious of the adventure. When you have slept through London air raids and inside a child's gas mask, you can sleep anywhere in Lancashire. Mum did the entire baby walking after that, the ten year old lad forced to seek alternative amusement such as 'knock down ginger' and throwing stones at people's windows.

A few years ago I visited Tod, as the locals call it, fruitlessly seeking my lovely café. As I stood in the car park recalling distant memories, another ten-year-old lad appeared. He was dressed in black with dark skin and eyes and a white top knot holding his uncut hair. I was transported back to my café; my lovely uncle worked as a guard on the railways and often spoke about 'darkies' he had met. I asked the boy if he knew where my café was. In his best North-country accent he said, "Yer standin' on it lass; they pulled it down to build t' cah pahk."

38 BELOW STAIRS

"I'm not well," I screamed, the two boys scattering to the safety of their rooms. They were growing up whilst their parents were falling down, or at least the marriage was. I tried my best to hide it which resulted in headaches, sleepless nights and frustration. We were nearing separation and I was heading for a breakdown. I tried deep breathing, praying, shouting and outbursts. I talked a lot on the phone but the neurosis was just under the surface. My sons accepted me as I was and knew when to keep quiet, back off or just endure.

This particular day it was all too much, I needed to let off steam. We lived beside a playing field. "I'll go to the middle and scream," I thought, but the vision of two hundred surrounding neighbours dialling 999 and alerting men in white coats to take me away prevented me from doing so. My second plan unfolded and I went in the cupboard under the stairs. I covered my mouth with a thick cushion and screamed long and loud until my throat was sore. It worked; I really did feel better. "Excellent," I exclaimed, "I shall do that again. Now I really must get on." I went to open the door; it was stuck.

I banged until my knuckles were stinging. My rasping voice, already weakened from screaming, gathered what remained of its strength to call for help. I yelled each boy's name in turn – nothing, so tried banging again. I was scared and began to panic in what appeared to be fast turning into a tomb. I imagined how the mummies must have felt surrounded by gold and jewels. "A lot different from me," I pondered, "I had tennis racquets, old shoes, the ends of coats ruffling my hair and oh my God, spiders! Please, please no spiders."

Arachnophobia set in, causing immense dread and a pressing need to free myself from this black enveloping chasm, swiftly engulfing me and ensuring I would never be seen again. I turned with my back to the door, my feet pushing against the gas and electricity metres. Where does strength come from when faced with impending death? The thought of suffocation and being found with a pale waxy skin painted by the grim reaper, enabled me to push with all my might against the wood and metal that was preventing me from living the rest of my life. I grunted, swore, heaved and banged against it.

Suddenly there was a crack of splitting wood; the door gave way and I fell into the hallway, still clutching my cushion. I lay there, exhausted but savouring the delight of my freedom, my breathing slowing to an even pace. My eldest son ran down the stairs, obviously alerted by the noise. He saw me, carefully stepping over on his way to the TV.

"Hello, Mum." No questions; unruffled by his prone mother, just another day living with a neurotic woman.

39 ASHES TO ASHES

Most people are sad at funerals, sometimes fearful of their own mortality. Sad, perhaps, because they are saying their last goodbye; but why do some people laugh and why are there so many funny stories associated with them?

He wanted to be buried at sea; too expensive so we would scatter his ashes off Bangor pier. It was a beautiful day, windy but sunny. As we walked along this lovely historic landing place, now refurbished and brightly painted with memorial seats and tiny booths, we felt an intense sadness, but it was a fitting end to a life working in Dickie's Boat Yard. We said what we thought were suitable words, opened the crimson biodegradable casket and emptied the contents into the Menai Straits. We smiled; his memory would always come back to us. Just as this thought floated away, the wind changed, bringing Uncle back quicker than expected and covering us in the grey ash that once was he!

There's a large Catholic church near my house; Catholic funerals are long. About five minutes in the other direction is a baker. Yesterday I watched four undertakers (must we now say funeral directors?) walking slowly back to the church, eating sausage rolls from paper bags and brushing the pastry crumbs from their neat black suits. It's only a job.

I begged an hour off work to go to my friend's funeral. I couldn't attend the wake so I said goodbye at the cemetery, got into my car and drove back to work. I parked outside, suddenly realising that the whole of the funeral procession had followed me for the party and were exiting their cars. I spent the next ten minutes redirecting them to the deceased's home.

Eddie's funeral was in southwest London; we had to follow the hearse along Putney High Street where there was a traffic jam. We sat, sad faced as the shoppers passed by, women discreetly bowing their heads, old men doffing their caps. Thirty minutes later, the same men passed by, unable to perform the same deferential movement as both hands were filled with Sainsbury's carrier bags. We had moved about six yards!

There were four of us and a crematorium official in a long black robe and pebble glasses. He was with us to inter the ashes in a prepared hole in the turf next to where mum was. We didn't know the procedure. I handed him the urn; my sister gave him a red rose to later be placed on the covered remains. Not realising we had not removed the thorns, he pricked his finger.

"Oh sh..." He just about managed to stop the whole word escaping. He bent forward at the knees, all of us simultaneously dipping and bowing reverently, preparing for the act of prayer.

Nothing happened so I sneaked a peep through my slightly opened lashes to see him wrapping his bleeding finger in a less than white handkerchief and muttering something about blood red roses; at least I think that's what I heard. We composed ourselves; he emptied the contents into the hole, dropping the urn and spilling some of the ashes, the wind sending some of them around our feet and attaching to my trouser legs. My poor sister started to shake; I stepped to her side to comfort her. When putting my arm around her shoulders I realised she was laughing uncontrollably with tears streaming down her cheeks. Regretfully we all ended up laughing, and Dad would have loved it. Unfortunately the man in black did not, patting the sod in place with his boot and storming off in the direction of the crematorium leaving us all holding on to each other in our laughter stricken grief.

My mum was a wonderful cook, always filling our bellies and often our freezers with cakes, pies and treats. It was fitting that we should have a splendid party after her funeral. It was a cold January day; the house was full with family and friends and we all ate well. Some few weeks before she died, she had presented me with an excellent cheesecake which I had frozen for a future occasion. This seemed just like the right occasion so I had defrosted it in the morning. Everyone enjoyed it; my cousin halfway through her second piece said, "This is absolutely beautiful, who made it?"

"Gran did," replied my son grinning.

My cousin exploded, showering me in cream and turning the colour of the cheesecake slowly slithering from her plate to the floor.

40 BUSINESS STUDIES

All of my life I worked in administration, learning to touch type on old manual typewriters with covers so that we could not see the keys. I progressed from 'dfghj' to 'asdfg' in a very short time. I moved on with technology, having one of the first electric typewriters in London in the early sixties to using prototype word processors in the early eighties. I love computers.

In the late eighties I took a job as an instructor at a training college for adults with disabilities, the trainees including some with mental health problems. The principal told me that I only had to show them what I had been doing all my life. I had no teaching experience and only two weeks training. Most of the time I was only two sheets ahead of my pupils, but I was the teacher, I was in charge. I had to appear knowledgeable and look authoritative.

There was one young man who tried every day to get the better of me and we often found ourselves in a confrontational situation. Many times I stood up to him, the voice of a giant hidden in my five foot frame. I found it preferable when having to chastise him, to do so whilst he was seated as he was six feet two inches and almost as wide.

I had full control of my seventeen male students, but he was always plotting to get one over on me, plans inside his head exposed through his piercing blue eyes. He had been unnervingly quiet in the morning and said nothing as we all went off for lunch. As we started the afternoon session, books and papers shuffled on tables; everyone chatted as I prepared my work and cleared the whiteboard.

"Right now, settle down," I commanded, waiting for the chatter to subside. I then used a rather prissy but authoritative voice to explain the lesson:

"This afternoon we are going to use the dictaphone."

Silence – then my young friend looked me straight in the eyes.

"I'd rather use my finger, Miss."

"Oh God, don't blush, don't blush, be in control, don't let him see he's got you."

Everyone sniggered. I took a deep breath. "As I said, this afternoon we are going to use the dictating machine."

The word dictaphone was never used again by any instructor.

41 CLOSE SHAVE

Our family of four lived in a two up, two down council house from the late forties until Mum and Dad left in the nineties. My dad worked all hours; my mum was an amazing manager of his meagre income, trying all sorts of ways to make it go further. The lavatory seat was old; they couldn't afford to replace it so she went to the ironmongers, purchasing some red varnish which she felt would complement the green distemper on the lavatory walls.

Dad did night work, sleeping during the day. She packed us off to school, read the Daily Sketch, did the crossword, had a cuppa and a quick roll-up and set to work painting the lavatory seat. 'Quick drying' it said on the tin, ensuring plenty of time before anyone needed to use it. She could use a 'Jerry' during the day if she had the call.

The size of the house prevented anyone being afforded their 'own space' and the only private time was spent in the lavatory. This was where I sang opera, my sister read comics and my dad studied form and caught up with the daily news. Time passed as we all used this tiny area to fulfil our fantasies in addition to carrying out the essential bodily functions. Dad loved the horses and dreamed of getting a 'double up' to supplement his small wages. This particular day he was up a little earlier whilst Mum was still at the shops and we hadn't come home. He retired to 'the room', read the front page and 'The Stars', saw what was on the radio and turned to the racing page. He didn't always bet but still tried to pick the winners each day.

I had been told that Dad's ancestors came from Spain. Although at that time he was very bald, photos had shown him at one time to have very dark locks. I had inherited black tresses, and later on, my sons carried on the family resemblance. The male members of my family often had to shave more than once a day and I followed with a history of depilation in the leg area and a covering of the Mediterranean moustache.

Back to the horses; Dad folded his paper, threw it to the floor and prepared to bend to retrieve his pants and braced trousers. He could not move; his backside stuck to the rim of the toilet seat. The more he tugged, the more pain he experienced. He was stuck in the fullest sense. My sister came home through the gate at the side of the house and in the back door. The smell of freshly baked jam tarts mixed with a pungent smell she didn't recognise. She picked up a tart on her way past and threw her coat and satchel on the settee in the front room. The crumbly pastry flecked her navy-blue uniform, waiting there to be used later as evidence against her fervent lies that she had not eaten a tart. With Mum not there, she popped her head around the hall door calling "Hallo" up the stairs.

Dad shouted, "Is that you, love?"

"It's me, Dad," she replied.

"Quick, love, find your Mum."

My sister ran out and up towards the shops to find Mum coming towards the house carrying her canvas shopping bag.

"Quick, Mum, Dad needs you."

I had now arrived home. Mum flew up the stairs, Dad letting her into the tiny room, the size necessitating that the door now be left open. My sister and I stood below awaiting some explanation; Mum ran down and past us.

"Was she smiling?" I asked my sister. She ran back with scissors in her hand. My darling dad had to be cut from his sticky prison cell.

"Go into the front room," Mum ordered, allowing Dad to retain his dignity and retrieve his attire.

Mum took a sheepish-looking Dad into the downstairs bathroom together with a large jar of her standby Vaseline. He returned some time later to the front room, sitting sideways on the settee whilst Mum explained what had happened. We all exploded, all except Dad that is. It took a long time for his skin to heal and for us to afford a new seat to replace that bright red and black furry item adorning the upstairs lavatory. In the meantime our various functions were carried out sitting directly on the very cold, white porcelain receptacle.

42 DRESS REHEARSAL

Uncle died in London, his only living relatives in Canada. His sister was in her seventies but felt the need to return and deal with all the items necessitated by a death; a need born out of their link with Mum and Dad now long gone and their childhood memories of the Depression.

She came with her daughter, my friend, leaving her elderly husband Joe in Ottawa. He was unhappy about her leaving, making it quite clear that he was unwell and it was her duty to stay with him. She was not moved by his protestations and arrived in our house on a Friday afternoon. Jet lag and the forthcoming weekend prevented any formal arrangements, so they planned a rest and perhaps a quick visit to Uncle's empty house.

On Saturday morning they went to Wandsworth, combining this with a quick visit to the West End. They had been gone about four hours when the phone rang in my house. It was my girlfriend's husband in Canada advising of the incredible news that Joe had died during the night and asking what on earth he should do!

How do you tell a woman visiting London to bury her brother that her husband has died in Canada?

Initially – panic. I then told my husband, who burst out laughing saying it was the best joke I had told him in ages. When he saw the look of dismay I displayed, his laughter dissolved and was replaced by a frozen stare

"How the heck are we going to tell her?" he asked me.

When the Canadians returned home, we made a great display of welcoming the mother; a bit over the top perhaps. We asked about the house, the changes she had seen in London, the shops. Anything to avoid her asking questions.

I took my girlfriend aside; she also laughed initially and then looked amazed that I could fabricate such a tale. When she realised the truth, she questioned how we would tell her mother about her stepfather. The important next step was to call Ottawa and suggest Joe be kept 'on ice' until we could get things sorted in London.

Arrangements for the UK funeral were made whilst many whisperings took place in various parts of our house. Once Mum had gone to bed, we sat with a bottle of wine and deliberated about how we could break the sad news. Some of the suggestions shown below may appear to be funny, sad or cruel, but they helped us get through a very difficult week.

"Morning, Mum, have you got used to the fact that Uncle has died? Well, here's another surprise!"

"You know the saying 'things only happen in threes'? We've just changed it to 'twos'."

"Have you heard the one about the family pet that died whilst they were on holiday?"

This one to be told after Uncle's funeral – "Did you enjoy that? Would you like another one?"

"Mum, you know sometimes people have wedding rehearsals. Have you ever heard of funeral rehearsals?"

Each night we tried to think of another, just to overcome the melancholy and it actually caused so much laughter. Fortunately as Mum was somewhat deaf, she missed it all! Transatlantic calls, however, brought us all down to earth.

We actually waited until after Uncle's funeral to impart the sad news. Obviously Mum was upset and very anxious to return to Canada, but her words were priceless: "The old bugger; he didn't want me to come to England. I bet he said to himself, 'I'll die, that'll teach her'."

43 LITTLE RED CAR

It was a small car; 'sewing machine on legs' was what one of the lads at worked called it. As my children became teenagers, one sat in front with the seat extended as far back as it would go whilst the other sat sideways on the back seat with his legs under his chin.

I worked in a sixteen storey building in south London and we used the multi-storey, circular car park next door. The lads in our department were good fun; we all got on well together and they could always be relied upon to help out in emergencies. I was a little late that day and had to park on the top floor. It was December; cold and a little icy. By 5:30 pm it was very icy and when I reached my tiny Fiat, it was frozen over. I could not undo the frozen locks to get my scraper. One of the lads came to my rescue; "I have a scraper". He set to and cleaned off all the windows whilst we chatted. I still couldn't open the doors.

Two more mates arrived, one with a lighter with which he warmed my car key and placed it inside the lock; still no luck. He tried the passenger side; nothing, it wouldn't budge. By now thirty minutes had passed.

"Shall I try to get in through the boot?" I asked.

"Good idea," he answered, his voice trembling with cold.

It began to snow. Lots of people had left, the lights in the adjacent building glowing now only on the floors where the cleaners were working. I worried about being late; this was the eighties, not the mobile phone age. If we couldn't succeed soon, I would have to go back into the building and call the kids.

I smiled at the lads as I walked to the rear of the car. I began to reach for the boot lock, bending forward to find the entry when I read the number plate. It was not my car; my little red Fiat was five cars further along!

When Shirley came out, she could drive off immediately, well, after a few brushes to remove the light snow.

I had to wait a little longer than her as I had to defrost my own car. I used the scraper he had thrown at me as he walked off in disgust.

44 SYRUPS

In the early sixties my friend lived in a London suburb. A group of young mums with pre-school children met regularly for coffee mornings where the women chatted and the children played. They became firm friends; the kids grew; coffee mornings became lunch sessions, and as time passed, dinner parties. No men were allowed, all having the pleasure of evening babysitting on these occasions.

As women do, they laughed a lot, told jokes, talked about their husbands and drank, cider mostly and perhaps some sherry. They each took turns to bring starters, main course and puddings, delighting in new recipes taken from women's magazines. Sometimes they held 'parties' where clothes, jewellery, and Tupperware were sold.

Quite often these gatherings followed a previous row in one of the homes and then comforting shoulders were offered; tears flowed and were quickly changed to laughter, everyone agreeing to criticise that particular pig of a husband. Sadly, no amount of advice, guidance or consolation could prevent the break-up of Joyce's marriage to Tony. Joyce moved back to her mum's with the girls, leaving Tony in the family home which was just across the road from Sarah. Sarah was able to regularly report any 'goings on'.

"I think someone has moved in," she said at one of the get-togethers.

Furious, Joyce told the others that whoever this woman was, she was not having the freezer that she had paid for. The freezer became subject of much discussion.

Some weeks later Sarah had a wig party. All shades, sizes and lengths of synthetic tresses were tried, the giggles increasing as the cider reached the spot. Although quite expensive, everyone decided to treat themselves and kept them on whilst they ate dinner. Again the discussion turned to the freezer and Joyce, having become more inebriated and less inhibited, decided that she would telephone her ex to discuss it. There was no one at home across the road.

The importance of this freezer reached immense proportions. As she still had a key, Joyce decided she would go across to the house and see if the freezer was still in the garage. The others would not let her go alone. Six very drunk women, heads covered in an assortment of wigs, crept across a suburban road in search of a freezer.

They reached the garage just as Tony arrived in his car. Suddenly the 'all for one, one for all' bond became 'abandon ship'. The five girls rushed in all directions, wigs flying, deserting their friend. Joyce, long blonde wig slightly askew, was drunkenly trying to explain what she was doing in her ex husband's garden. The last they heard, "Give me my key".

"No, you give me my freezer."

None of the girls were ever seen wearing a wig again.

45 SINS OF THE FATHERS

My sister was sixteen; she had not long left school and worked in a bank as a comptometer operator, a left handed one at that. A young man who worked in the Post Office tried very hard to get her to go out with him, and after some time, she agreed.

He was a little older, earned a little more and took her to the West End to see 'Fings Aint Wot They used to be'; they had really good seats and an exciting evening.

They travelled home by tube to the end of the northern line, laughing and trying to sing the songs from the show. This young gentleman saw her to the door and she asked him in for a coffee.

Our front door lead straight into our front room. Mum looked up from her usual place at the table.

"Mum, this is J..."; the sentence was unfinished.

The kitchen door burst open. Our Dad appeared with a huge boiling pan on his head, the handle pointing forward; a towel covering his lower half and two saucepan lids hanging from string around his neck and covering his hairy chest.

Needless to say my sister never saw this young man again and we often wondered what antics our parents got up to whilst we were out.

46 HAPPIEST DAYS?

At the age of sixty I felt that I had passed through all my baptisms of fire. I had been bullied at school. Before the age of eleven, this took the form of verbal abuse, loud chanting of rude remarks by a group of children. At eleven years old and in a single sex grammar school, the bullying was quieter, more subtle. This was perhaps more frightening as not obvious, not out in the open. I believed I had dealt with it; as an adult when teaching adults with problems, I was more aware and felt it helped me do a better job.

I had a call from an old school friend with whom I had lost touch almost forty years before. She was inviting me to attend a school reunion and asked me if I could make a list of the girls in my class. Sadly, the only names that came to mind were those of the two bullies, stirring up problems long since buried. I wrote a poem about my feelings and this acted to cathartically dispel those long-held horrors. I became excited by the forthcoming event and felt that my final reparation would be to tackle the two offenders.

They didn't come!

Everyone was disappointed and asked if anyone knew of their whereabouts, hoping by the next get together they might be found.

They did not arrive the next year, these two stars who everyone admired. They were smart, intelligent, good looking, and popular but they were also secret bullies.

At our lunch table I told of the bullying, everyone pressing me to know who had been so cowardly. I did not divulge the names at that time. In a later telephone conversation I told them to my friend, who was shocked to hear that these two school champions had a darker side to them.

I really don't care now, they have been exposed and even they are not aware. It is retribution enough.

47 TURNING THE TABLES

Life after separation is tough; even tougher when you are trying to keep a full time job and have two teenage children. The entire trauma that went before the separation still floats about in the back of your mind. The guilt accompanying a family break-up sometimes rises to the surface causing imbalance which manifests at best as edginess, at worst neurosis or complete mania. You do your best to keep on top but there are occasions that send you over the edge.

One such occasion was at the end of a particularly hard day when in addition to work, shopping, washing, cooking and ironing, I had to help my young son with his homework, maths for goodness sake! He had left it to the last minute; combining this with the last dregs of my daily energy, guaranteed an imminent explosion.

I couldn't do it for him; really I couldn't do it at all. He wouldn't try, he wouldn't listen. Tempers boiled, but I should have known better; he was just a child, but he wouldn't damn well listen!

The law of averages assured disaster. What was the probability of someone receiving a thick ear? If he had started the work just a fraction earlier, would the result have been different? I tried to calm down, tried to get him to listen. I was almost at breaking point; my hand rose in the air poised to land but no, I did not hit him. Instead I picked up his maths book and ripped it in half and half again.

He was dumbstruck for a few seconds, and then realising the enormity of it and the possibility of having to go to the lesson with no homework done and a shredded book, he started to jump around the room. By this time I was calm, the ripping action having found expression for my anger. I then set about trying to calm him, assuring all the while that it would be OK. After a half an hour of bonding, I sent him off to bed, telling him that I would sort it out and he accepted this.

The next hour was spent employing care mixed with Sellotape to repair the book. After a night's sleep and breakfast, I accompanied my son to school, leaving him in the playground. I then crept, like a naughty schoolgirl, to the maths teacher's room, to confess my actions. At future PTA meetings, Mr. Maths sat opposite me mouthing the words "Maths book" and smiling. To this day, almost twenty years later, I still cannot live it down.

48 SEXY SAGA

We were middle aged, both divorced and went on holiday to Portugal. It was October, beautiful weather, and at the small hotel, we had been unable to collect our key, being asked to come back at about four o'clock.

We went into the little town where we had coffee and bought some big, green juicy grapes and ate the lot between us. We sat at the edge of the sea watching the waves and ambled slowly back to the hotel. The foyer was crowded.

"There seem to be quite a number of older people," I said, "A lot of women".

Suddenly a buxom blonde girl of about thirty clapped her hands to gain attention when about thirty shades of grey heads turned in unison. Everything went quiet.

"Good afternoon everyone, I'm Davina. I'm your rep whilst you're here; anything you want, please ask. Perhaps we can start by warming up with a little of the local wine, compliments of the house."

As the wine was poured, taken and sipped, Davina started again

"Just a few preliminaries and you can get on with enjoying your holiday. As we are late on in the season, the sun should not be too hot; you need not go overboard with the sun tan lotion but take care at midday. Please don't eat the local fruit, especially grapes, without first washing them."

Rule number one broken!

"As you are all over pensionable age, I won't go into my usual 18-30's stuff about practising safe sex." The seniors tittered. I turned to my partner

"We're not over pensionable age; what's she talking about?" He blushed.

Rule number two broken!

We had booked in to a pensioners' holiday hotel. After some 'housekeeping' tips, Davina continued. "I think the easiest thing I can do now is to wish you all a very happy stay here and again, if there is anything you need, please ask me. I shall be here each morning at nine-thirty. Now your keys." She commenced reading from a list.

"Mr. and Mrs. Reynolds, number 20. Mr. and Mrs. Palmer, number 22. Miss Taylor and Mrs. Salmon, number 14." The list went on for a while, and then in what seemed to be a much louder voice, "Mr. Williams and Mrs. Brown in number 16."

All talking stopped, heads turned. My partner inched forward to collect the key, later telling me that he felt he was part of the French Revolution going through a baying crowd to the guillotine. Davina winked and gave him the key. We collected our cases and retreated to our room, the distant whispers sending us on our sinful way.

We fell on to the bed laughing, vowing not to let this spoil the vacation.

The best part was breakfast each morning where again we had to run the gauntlet to reach our table, passing nods, knowing smiles, grins, sneers and blank stares.

My partner took great delight each morning asking me in a loud voice, "Do you take sugar?"

49 JERSEY

My cousin in Jersey has just died making the 'front line' at the head of my family a little thinner. I first went to Jersey in 1949. I travelled with Mum, Dad and my sister on a boat from Weymouth and it took seven hours. My sister was sick all the way there and then all the way home again. At that time we stayed with my aunt and uncle with whom I had lived in Lancashire and who had immigrated to the island after the war. They were such happy holidays; we laughed a lot.

We spent afternoons on the beach, just five of us and perhaps a couple of people walking the dog; glorious days, full of sun and fun. I have a photo of me walking along the promenade holding an inflatable rubber ring on one arm and my towel folded with cosie inside and tucked under the other arm.

The entertainment was simple and we were such a happy bunch, Mum and her cousin always finding something to laugh about. One windy day my rubber ring blew away with all of us chasing it along the walkway; every time it came within grasp, the wind lifted it out of reach. The spectacle of Dad and me running, bending, grabbing and missing started group laughter which was infectious. Mum could not stop the hysteria acting on her weak bladder, and with no public toilet in sight, she stood over a drain in the pavement relieving herself of the problem. Having captured the ring and settled on the beach, she washed her knickers in the sea and we carried on with our planned afternoon.

There were Jersey milk bars where you could buy thick, frothy milkshakes and a hot doughnut shop. We stayed in a cottage with no running water and an outside toilet shared with another family. Cut up squares of daily paper hung on a nail on the old, cold stone wall, deputising as toilet paper and a little reading matter. There was always a damp, musty smell; the buildings were very old.

This was in the days long before Jersey became a tax haven. Now we stay in hotels with not only running water, but en suite in every room and two swimming pools.

50 JERSEY NOW

We travelled the car park lift in Bromley with our granddaughter, aged two, in her buggy. Granddad wanted to make her laugh so he sang, danced and jumped up and down; the lift jammed! We pressed the emergency button and waited a while when we heard the clanging of a fire engine bell, the brigade coming to the rescue. Our little girl was so excited; I was very embarrassed.

Later that year we were in a hotel in Jersey, my husband relating the tale to my sister. We got into the lift to go down for dinner.

"How on earth did it jam?" she asked.

"I jumped," replied my husband, jumping again.

History repeats itself – the lift jammed again. We pressed the emergency button; this time no firemen. We waited an age, but eventually the janitor forced open the door. We were halfway between the first floor and the lobby. As the door opened, we were greeted by the janitor and receptionist, but behind them, seated in a row and awaiting the dinner call, were six Chelsea pensioners, resplendent in their scarlet uniforms and really enjoying the performance.

We all had to jump six feet to the lobby floor, and I vowed never again to take a lift with my husband.

51 MOTHER KNOWS BEST

A family party; lots of people feasting after the wedding mass. Suits and loosened ties, newly pressed shirts, large flouncy hats, some now removed and occupying chairs as if hiding tiny leprechauns beneath. Yes, an Irish wedding, in Harlow.

Gammy as she was called by her twelve grandchildren, was listening to a conversation, selective deafness working in her favour as usual. All of her seven boys and girls were scattered around the room, her eldest grandson, the bridegroom, looking a little thoughtful. She knew he missed his Poppa on this very special day. Poppa had been gone two years now.

Her daughter Sheelagh came and sat beside her.

"What are they talking about Ma?"

"Oral sex" was the reply.

Her daughter, surprised by her mother's openness said, "Oh and what is that then, Ma?"

"For goodness sake girl, do you know nothing. It's when people talk about it!"

Her daughter could not contain herself; the group of sisters and granddaughters nearby erupted on receiving an explanation. One of the granddaughters, who did not like to see her Gamma being ridiculed, sat beside her and gently told her the true meaning. Gamma looked shocked and loudly said, "Oh, how dreadful. I should be absolutely disgusted if any of my girls did that."

Sheelagh looked up and said, "Oh God, I wished she'd told us that a long time ago."

52 EVENIN' ALL

We lived in Clapham Junction; my husband was a newly recruited Police Constable. I travelled by train to Waterloo and back, arriving back at the junction at about 6 pm. When my young copper was on the late shift, I always looked out for him when walking home. This was the early sixties when policemen were everywhere and always in pairs.

I forgot to mention, I am short sighted and vain! I would not wear my distance glasses outside, then or now.

Exiting the station I always recognised the dark blue uniform and distinctive helmet in the distance. I often ran towards the PC calling "Oooh, oooh" or sometimes whistling, a very unlady-like habit I still practise. I would grab hold of his arm, regularly attempting to plant a kiss. They all looked the same to me.

Nine times out of ten it wasn't him, but I soon got to know all the coppers on that shift!

53 APRIL FOOL

1st April 1982, Colliers Wood, South London; if you know this area you will recognise the tall grey building, all sixteen floors of it. At that time it housed a large company constructing oil rigs and where just over four hundred people worked.

At around 8:45 am, the lifts were always very busy. I entered the building this particular morning, pressed number fifteen and my fellow travellers pressed their respective floor numbers. The lift climbed and at the fourth floor the door opened. The passenger alighted looking up at the brass number plate on the opposite wall, saw 'three' and jumped back into the lift.

The next chosen floor was 'seven'; the lift stopped at this floor where the brass plate showed 'nine' and again a surprised occupant got back into the lift. Now all the passengers were looking quizzically at each other.

The lift rose automatically to fifteen and when I exited, the plate showed 'eleven'. By the time I had realised, the door had closed so I decided to walk. I opened the door to the stair well ready to climb four floors. To my surprise there was only one flight and I was on the sixteenth floor.

I descended to my office on the floor below where all the girls were discussing their journey in the lift. Complete chaos.

Someone had been in very early in the morning and changed all the floor numbers.

54 SUPER MAN!

The Christmas party was to be fancy dress, so my son and a girl colleague visited the party shop at lunch time. The only costume in his size was 'Superman' so he took it into the cubicle to try on.

The tight fit of the trousers necessitated the removal of his boxer shorts. He affixed the cape and there being no mirror, he stepped outside the cubicle, did a twirl and standing, legs spread apart, tall and proud with his hands on his hips, he asked, "What about this then?"

Sadly my son had not noticed the split in the front of the costume to enable calls of nature to be taken. His companion's reply, which was accompanied by a slight blush and a glance at the open fly was, "Oh boy, really <u>super</u> man, but doesn't he always wear his pants on the outside of his trousers?"

55 SHEENA

I was teaching business studies to a group of beautiful young adults with disabilities. One of the ways to encourage communication was to discuss embarrassing moments, and I always started. My story was of leaving a group of students reading whilst I went to the ladies and coming back with my skirt tucked in my knickers and dragging a few yards of pink toilet paper in my wake. This always broke the ice.

Sheena was pretty, intelligent, humorous, loving and with a progressive illness. She never lost her temper, worked hard at everything. A lovely young woman and an inspiration. Her embarrassing moment was from her school days and this was how she told it.

"I was in the middle of a particularly boring physics lesson on a very hot day. The teacher's voice was soothing; I nodded off and really didn't know for how long. I awoke suddenly hearing the teacher calling my name and telling me to go to the back of the class, stand and clap. I thought this was a very strange request but made my way to the back, stood and clapped for some time. The teacher shouted at me to stop and then asked what on earth I thought I was doing. I said I was doing what she had asked me to – go to the back, stand and clap.

The class collapsed with loud laughter echoing around the room. The teacher also laughed saying, 'Sheena, for goodness sake, I said go to the back of the class and get a stand and a clamp'."

56 MUSIC HALL

Television is not an important part of my life, music is. The 'wireless' was always on in our house. Until we were old enough to buy records and answer back, we listened mostly to what Dad and Mum chose.

We moved to London from Medway when I was seven, almost eight. I do, however, have a vivid memory before that time of a visit to Chatham Empire, sitting in the balcony, watching a sand dance performed by Wilson, Keppell and Betty. I don't know if it would be PC nowadays. We tried it on our garden path, shuffling behind each other on some grit nicked from a pile in the road.

I am still thrilled by live stage musicals, a love passed down through the generations from my parents to my grandchildren. Long may live theatre continue.

57 SEQUINES

I started dancing at the age of ten when we all wore black shoes with metal taps and practised 'shuffle hop stamp stamp' on a Saturday morning in the drill hall. From there I progressed to ballroom dancing lessons and the occasional old thyme dances.

If you ever visit Blackpool Tower Ballroom, although perhaps now a little shabby, listen for the echoes of a time since past and you will hear the strains of the organ accompanied by the distant pride of a twelve-year-old girl dancing the Velita and St Bernard's Waltz with an equally proud dad.

At fifteen, a more deviant pastime of rock roll. At seventeen, back to the ballroom and at twenty-one, I married a man who could not dance, finding foot coordination rather difficult. He was, however, in that state of love which causes one to agree to things which in a more sane state of mind, would not be tolerated. He agreed to take dancing lessons and paid for a course at the Victor Sylvester Ballroom in Wimbledon. The course ended just before Christmas, celebrated by a full-blown dance party to which friends and family were invited.

My first mistake was to request a little rock and roll and ask if the teacher had any Bill Hayley records. She reluctantly agreed that we might have a jive just before the last waltz. There was an interval during which we all sat around the edge of the dance floor on wine coloured, velveteen topped seats. Being newly married and so very much in love with this wonderful man who had tried so hard to learn to dance, I sat on his lap and gazed lovingly into his eyes, unaware of the room, the time or anyone around us.

Suddenly I was jolted out of my fairy tale by a fierce tap on my shoulder. I turned quickly to see the dance teacher

"Get orff," she commanded.

"But we're married," I stuttered, shocked at her loud and bitter voice.

"I don't care what you are, get orff, we do not do that sort of thing at Victor Sylvester's."

We were all very careful not to get too close during the last waltz which, if had been down the road at the Palais, it would have been much more steamy and would have sent Miss 'Side Close Side' into an hysterical frenzy.

58 PROJECTION

All of my dreams, my fantasies, my tales of undying love and passion, were fashioned in the dark of the Gaumont. I didn't care if Alan Ladd stood on a box to kiss the leading lady; I didn't know anyway. I saw *Seven Brides for Seven Brothers* fifteen times, often twice through. The showings in the fifties were continuous and no one minded if you stayed on to see the programme again.

Kirk Douglas affected my hormone level and I could sing all the songs from any musical, my range encompassing Howard Keel's deep notes and flying up to 'Wash that man right out of my hair'.

I started out at Saturday morning pictures, following the words on the screen at the front. "We come along on Saturday morning, greeting everybody with a smile". Sadly this philosophy was not followed by the boy who hit me over the head with a lemonade bottle (glass in those days), nor to the girl who stuck chewing gum in my long tresses, necessitating an instant shortening when I arrived home.

Sometimes we would go to the pictures as a family, Mum, Dad and my sister meeting me off the bus from school. We had a picnic of cheese sandwiches, home made cake and tea from a flask, all devoured automatically in the dark whilst Dirk Bogarde was preparing to 'knock off' PC49 or 'The Deadwood Stage was coming up over the hill'.

There was always an interval between the 'B' and 'A' films and when Mum and Dad could afford it, us two girls would have an ice cream served by an usherette holding a torch which she shone in her tray to make sure she gave the correct change. If I step into the revolving door which enters the maze of my past, I can feel the small block, covered in ice cold paper and accompanied by two wafers. What did Mum go without to let us have such a treat?

I have a small insignificant mole above my lip on the right side of my face. How many times was this enhanced with an eyebrow pencil whilst staring into my bedroom mirror pretending to be Margaret Lockwood, praying that the fiercely attractive James Mason would break down my bedroom door, take off his mac and his trilby and 'Dim lights; fade screen, title music and credits'.

What would he do to me?

I was saddened recently to be told by a friend who was a little older than me that she had no memories of the pictures. She had heard the term 'first house and second house'. She thought these were the two picture houses she passed on her way to school.

This black and white tapestry enlarged and enriched my mind and gave me the thirst for more cinematic experiences still enjoyed today.

59 INTIMACY

Sixteen months into widowhood I was called for a routine smear test. The receptionist was very discreet, whispering over the telephone.

"Do you still have periods? Can you bring a sample?", and much quieter, "No sexual intercourse for 48 hours prior to the examination."

"Chance would be a fine thing," I wanted to reply.

I repeated this experience to my sister and we laughed together. She suggested I might "ask for it on prescription."

When I went for the test, I was going to recount the tale to the nurse but as she was only about 12-years-old and saw me as she would see her grandmother, I thought better of it.

As she was new to the practise she had to have a GP in attendance and requested I prepare myself whilst she called a woman doctor.

I lay on the couch, with a strategically placed piece of paper and nothing on the bottom half except my black socks. The doctor appeared through the curtain, smiled, looked amazed and said, "Oooh, how wonderful!"

Before I could gather my surprise, she continued, "Your lipstick matches your top!"

60 FRIENDS

I had been a widow for approximately 7 months when I had a call from Australia asking me to attend a family wedding in Bali. I was not strong; I wanted to say "no". I was frightened to leave the safety of my own home, but I said "yes". It was what my husband would have done.

I spent a few days in Hong Kong and then travelled to Bali where I met the family and prepared to spend a week. I stayed separately, ensuring that they did not feel they had to look after me. The hotel was beautiful in the Balinese style; small, comfortable and I was very well looked after by a young male housekeeper who came in twice each day, the second visit to turn down the bedcovers, often leaving a flower on my pillow.

My family visited me on the second day and as it was so hot, left their drinks in my fridge. As they were about to leave, they remembered the water and my nephew ran to my room to collect it. When he came back he told me he had seen the housekeeper. When I returned to the room the housekeeper told me he had seen my friend.

I thought no more about it until later in the evening when I got back to my room and found both sides of the bed had been turned down with flowers on each pillow. He had thought that my nephew was a really good friend!

I made a point the next day of introducing the housekeeper to my nephew's wife and that evening only one side of the bed was turned down!

Printed in the United Kingdom
by Lightning Source UK Ltd.
100186UKS00001B/172-189